**"You're welcome t[...]
you like."**

"I like that idea." Tammy rose on tiptoe and pressed her lips to his. He wrapped his arms around her and turned it into a proper kiss.

They pulled apart. "Why don't I follow you home?" she said and reached for her car door. She immediately recoiled and let out a moan.

"What is it?" Vince took her arm. "What's wrong?"

She pointed, and now he saw that something red was smeared across the car door and across the windshield. He leaned around to examine the windshield and went cold all over when he read the message scrawled in the same red across the glass: *Next time you won't be so lucky. V.*

TWIN JEOPARDY

CINDI MYERS

Harlequin
INTRIGUE

To Gini

 **Harlequin®**
INTRIGUE™

ISBN-13: 978-1-335-45711-0

Twin Jeopardy

Copyright © 2024 by Cynthia Myers

 Harlequin Enterprises ULC
22 Adelaide St. West, 41st Floor
Toronto, Ontario M5H 4E3, Canada
www.Harlequin.com

Printed in Lithuania

MIX
Paper | Supporting responsible forestry
FSC® C021394

Cindi Myers is the author of more than seventy-five novels. When she's not plotting new romance storylines, she enjoys skiing, gardening, cooking, crafting and daydreaming. A lover of small-town life, she lives with her husband and two spoiled dogs in the Colorado mountains.

Books by Cindi Myers

Harlequin Intrigue

Eagle Mountain: Criminal History

Mile High Mystery
Twin Jeopardy

Eagle Mountain: Critical Response

Deception at Dixon Pass
Pursuit at Panther Point
Killer on Kestrel Trail
Secrets of Silverpeak Mine

Eagle Mountain Search and Rescue

Eagle Mountain Cliffhanger
Canyon Kidnapping
Mountain Terror
Close Call in Colorado

Eagle Mountain: Search for Suspects

Disappearance at Dakota Ridge
Conspiracy in the Rockies
Missing at Full Moon Mine
Grizzly Creek Standoff

Visit the Author Profile page at Harlequin.com.

CAST OF CHARACTERS

Tammy Patterson—The reporter for the *Eagle Mountain Examiner* knows what it's like to lose someone she loves. When she sets out to write a feature about the disappearance of a girl fifteen years before, she has no idea how personal the mystery will become for her.

Vince Shepherd—After seeing how hard volunteers worked to find his twin sister when she went missing when he was ten, Vince vowed to one day join search and rescue and help others. He also hopes the volunteer work will lead him to finding his sister someday.

Valerie Shepherd—Vince's twin disappeared on a camping trip in the mountains when the siblings were only ten. The mystery of what happened to her has haunted the family.

Mitch Patterson—Tammy's brother is a successful real estate agent and her closest confidant.

Elizabeth Rollins—Mitch Patterson's new girlfriend is everything Tammy is not—tall, gorgeous, poised and wealthy. But is Tammy's dislike of the woman all due to jealousy?

Bethany Ames—The newest search and rescue volunteer has taken a keen interest in Vince. She always seems to be around when disaster strikes.

Chapter One

"Look right down there in that gully. Just to the left of that tree branch that's sticking up out of the gravel. See that flash of white? I'm sure that's bones."

Eagle Mountain Search and Rescue volunteer Vince Shepherd moved in closer beside the couple who had summoned the team to this remote mountain trail above Galloway Basin. He squinted toward the spot the man had indicated. Yes, that definitely looked like a long bone. A femur, maybe? And was that a rib cage? His heart pounded with a mixture of hope and fear.

"They sure look human to me," the female half of the pair, a sturdy brunette who wore her hair in a long braid, said.

Search and rescue captain Danny Irwin lowered the binoculars he had focused on whatever was down there in the gully. "It's worth checking out," he said. "Thanks for calling it in."

"Looks like a pretty gnarly climb down there." The male hiker, red-haired and red-bearded, frowned into the gully. "Lots of downed trees and loose rock."

"We'll figure it out," Danny said. Tall and lanky, with shaggy brown hair and a laconic manner, in another context he might have been mistaken for a surfer instead of a registered nurse and search and rescue veteran. He looked past them to the gathered volunteers—only six responders, since this had been deemed a nonemergency call and not everyone was free on a Friday morning. "Three of us will make the hike down," he said. "The other three need to monitor the situation up top, in case any of us get into trouble."

"I'll go down with you." Vince stepped forward. He was one of the newer members of the group, but he had done a lot of hiking and climbing before he joined up, and he wanted to get a closer look at those bones. Part of him dreaded seeing them, but better to know the truth sooner rather than later. It was a long shot that those bones had anything to do with his sister, but what if they really did belong to her?

"I'll go too," Hannah Gwynn said. A paramedic, Hannah served as the team's current medical officer.

"If you hike down from the top end of the gulley, it's not that steep." Sheri Stevens, on summer vacation from her teaching position, looked up the mountainside. "You won't need to rope up or anything."

"Yeah, we just have to pick our way around the dead trees, boulders and loose gravel swept down by spring run-off," Danny said. He looked to Vince. "You ready to go?"

"Yeah."

They left Sheri, along with Grace Wilcox and Caleb Garrison, to monitor the situation up top. The hikers who had called in the find elected to head back down the mountain. Danny led the way, picking a path through the debris-choked gully. The July sun beat down, but at this high elevation the warmth was welcome. Wildflowers carpeted the meadows alongside the gully, and if it weren't for the reason for their presence here, it would have been an enjoyable outing. The climb wasn't physically challenging, but it was tedious and frustrating, requiring frequent backtracking and constant readjustments to the unsteady footing. "How did those bones ever end up down here?" Vince wondered out loud as he clambered over a fallen tree trunk, then skirted a large boulder.

"They might have washed down from farther up the mountain," Hannah said. She hopped over a mudhole, then pulled aside a fallen branch to clear a better path.

Danny stopped to gauge their progress, then pulled out his handheld radio. "How much farther do we have to go?" he asked.

"You've got about five hundred feet," Sheri replied. "You'll know you're close when you see that big branch sticking up. It's got most of the bark peeled off of it. The bones are just beyond that."

"I may need you to direct us when we get there," Danny said. "There's so much debris down here it's hard to distinguish details."

They squeezed through a tangle of tree limbs, then trudged across a section of mud, boots sinking with each step, before scaling a jumble of granite slabs. "Guess I'm getting my workout in for the day," Vince said, as he hauled himself to the top of what he hoped was the final slab. From here, he had a view down the gully. "I think that's the tree Sheri was talking about." He pointed toward a jagged branch, the bare wood shining white in the sun.

"I see a path through to there," Danny said. He hopped down from the slab and set out again, shoving aside knots of brush as he went. Hannah followed, with Vince bringing up the rear.

"You're almost there," Sheri radioed. "Look uphill."

A few minutes later, Danny stopped. "We're here," he said, and crouched down to examine something on the ground.

Vince hung back. "Is it human bones?" he called.

Hannah moved in closer and leaned over Danny's shoulder. "It's a skeleton, all right," she said. "Kind of small. Maybe a child?"

For a moment, Vince stopped breathing. Valerie had been ten when she disappeared from the family's campsite above

Galloway Basin. A four-foot dynamo with sandy-brown curls cut short, she had a dimple in her left cheek that matched Vince's own. He forced himself to move forward until he was standing beside Hannah, looking down on a small rib cage, and a heap of arm and leg bones.

Danny moved up the gully a few steps and began shifting a pile of rocks. After a few seconds, he stood once more. "It's not a human," he said. "It's a bear."

"What?" Hannah looked up from her scrutiny of the bones.

"The skull is right here." Danny pulled out something from among the rocks and held it up. The skull was oblong, with a prominent jaw, one oversize canine tooth jutting from one corner of the mouth.

"A bear?" Vince staggered a little. Not Valerie.

"Kind of a small one." Danny leaned over the skeleton once more. "See, if you look closer, you can tell the femur is too short to be human, and the shoulder blades are a lot wider."

"You're right," Hannah said. "I guess I was thinking 'human' because that's what the hikers called in, and at first glance it's similar."

"Maybe a cub that didn't make it through a hard winter," Danny said.

Vince was dimly aware of their conversation. A bear. Not a little girl. Not Valerie.

"It really did look like a human from a distance." Hannah hugged her elbows. "I can't say I'm sorry we don't have to try to transport a skeleton out of here."

Danny dropped the skull. "That's it, then. Let's get away from here." He pulled out his radio. "We're headed back up," he said. "The bones weren't human, but a bear's."

Hannah started to move past Vince but stopped. "Are you okay?" she asked. "You look like you don't feel so hot."

"I'll be okay." He ran his hand over his face. "I guess I was trying to prepare myself for the worst, and now…"

Hannah's eyes widened. She gripped his shoulder. "Oh my gosh, Vince. I didn't even think! You thought this was Valerie, didn't you?"

No sense lying about it. "I knew it probably wasn't," he said. "But our camp wasn't that far from here, and after all these years, we're still waiting for her to be found."

Danny had ended his radio transmission and joined them. "Is something wrong?" he asked.

Hannah squeezed Vince's arm. "I'm sorry," she said. "I should have remembered."

"No reason you should have," he said. "It was a long time ago." Fifteen years. Most of his life.

Danny was watching him, a puzzled look on his face. "Something I need to know about?" he asked.

"My sister." Vince cleared his throat and focused on pulling himself together. After this long, he hadn't expected to feel so emotional. "My twin sister. She disappeared on a family camping trip in the mountains the summer we were ten." He looked past Danny, toward the mountains rising around them. "Not that far from here. She was never found, so when I heard bones had been spotted up here, I couldn't help wondering…" His voice trailed away.

"That's rough," Danny said. "Do you have any idea what happened to her?"

"None. Maybe she fell or had some other kind of accident, but lots of people looked, for days, and we never found any sign of her."

"I was a little older than you, but I still remember the posters around town and people volunteering to help search," Hannah said. "It really is scary how someone can just vanish up here."

"Sometimes they get found years later," Danny said. "There

was that woman about ten years ago. She had disappeared skiing three years before, and her remains were found in a bunch of avalanche debris."

"You must think about Valerie every time you're up here," Hannah said.

"I do," Vince said. "And pretty much every time I'm up here, I look for her." Though that wasn't the sole reason he had joined search and rescue, it had been one consideration.

"I hope someone finds your sister one day," Hannah said. "I'm sorry it wasn't today."

"Really, I'm okay now. It was just kind of a shock." He shrugged, trying to appear steadier than he felt. "Like you said, now we don't have to haul a body bag up out of this gully." He didn't wait for them to answer, but turned and began retracing his steps. For a brief moment, when he had first looked down on those bones, a wave of dizziness washed over him, a mixture of profound relief that they would finally know Valerie's fate and gut-wrenching grief at proof that she really was gone. No matter how improbable it would be for her to still be alive after all this time, as long as they didn't have a body, they were able to cling to a sliver of hope that she was still walking around somewhere and maybe one day they would be reunited.

Finding out the bones weren't even human resulted in the kind of nausea-inducing whiplash experienced on roller coasters and bungee jumps. A few deep breaths and a little physical exertion, and he'd be all right again. Valerie was still gone. Probably dead. They would likely never know what happened to her. It was a reality he had grown used to, even if he had never fully accepted it.

"I HAVE AN idea for a series of articles I want to do." Tammy Patterson, the *Eagle Mountain Examiner*'s only full-time reporter, stood in front of editor Russ Saunders's desk, notepad in hand. Russ cast a jaundiced eye on anything he considered "too fluffy," so she would have to pitch this right.

Russ removed the cigar from the corner of his mouth— he never smoked the things, just chewed them. Tammy suspected he had adopted the habit when he first took helm of the paper when he was fresh out of college, thinking it made him appear more mature and even jaded. Now he actually was mature—north of fifty—and definitely jaded. "What's your idea?" he asked.

"This year is the twenty-fifth anniversary of the founding of Eagle Mountain Search and Rescue," she said. "I want to run a series of articles that looks back on some of their most dramatic callouts and daring rescues."

"Why would our readers care?" This was the question he always asked.

"People love reading about local heroism, not to mention danger, the outdoors and even unsolved mysteries."

"How is this going to contribute to our bottom line?" This was Russ's other favorite question, and one she had also anticipated.

"We'll ask local businesses to buy space for messages or special ads that celebrate Eagle Mountain Search and Rescue's anniversary. They get to advertise their business and support a favorite local organization."

He leaned forward, elbows on the desk. "How many articles are you talking about?" he asked.

"Six. One every other week for three months."

She could practically see him running through the calculations in his head. "When can you have the first article ready?" he asked.

"Two weeks. I want to start with the search for Valerie Shepherd." Before he could ask, she rushed on. "She was a ten-year-old girl who disappeared on a family camping trip in the mountains fifteen years ago. Never a trace of her seen again. Search and rescue was part of the largest wilderness search in local history. That search really ushered in a new era for the group, with a turn toward more professional training and organization."

"I remember," Russ said. "Local family. Wasn't she a twin?"

"Yes. Her brother, Vince, works for the county Road and Bridge Department. Her parents are in Junction."

"You'll talk to them for your article."

"Of course. And search and rescue has agreed to give me access to their archives. And there are lots of photos in our files we can use."

"Sounds good," Russ said. "But don't let this take precedence over your regular news coverage."

"When have I ever done that, Russ?"

He chomped down on the cigar once more and spoke around it. "You're not a slacker, I'll give you that."

Smiling to herself, Tammy moved back to her desk. Working for the only paper in town, which came out once a week, was a great way to feel like she always knew everything going on. But the sameness of reporting on the school board and county commissioner's meetings, as well as perennial wrangles over building codes or the budget amount to devote to promoting tourism, could get old. It was good to have something exciting and interesting to write about. The fifteen-year-old mystery of a missing girl definitely wasn't going to be boring.

Chapter Two

"You're Vince Shepherd, right?"

Vince accepted the beer from the bartender at Mo's Pub and turned to see who was addressing him. A young woman with a cascade of blond curls and a friendly smile eyed him through round wire-rimmed glasses. "I'm Vince," he said, wary. "Who are you?"

"I'm Tammy Patterson. I'm a reporter for the *Eagle Mountain Examiner*." She offered her hand, nails polished bright pink and a trio of rings on her fingers.

"Sure. I've read your stuff." He shook her hand. What did a reporter want with him?

"Do you have a minute to talk?" she asked.

He sipped the beer. "Talk about what?"

"I'm working on a series of stories about Eagle Mountain Search and Rescue, to celebrate their twenty-fifth anniversary. I have a few questions for you."

"Okay. Sure." He could talk about search and rescue.

"There's a spot over here where it's a little quieter." She led the way to a booth near the back of the crowded bar.

"I haven't been with the group that long," Vince said as he slid into the padded seat across from her.

"What group is that?" she asked. She was searching in an oversize black leather tote bag.

"Search and rescue. You said you were writing about them."

"Oh. I didn't know you were a member of SAR." She pulled out a notepad, a pen and a small recorder and laid them on the table in front of her. "That's even better."

He sipped more beer and frowned. "If you didn't know I was with SAR, why do you want to talk to me?"

"I want to talk to you about your sister. Valerie."

Valerie again. It wasn't that he never thought about his missing twin, but after fifteen years she wasn't on his mind every day. But today she had taken up a disproportionate space in his head, what with the callout about the bones that morning. And now this reporter was asking about her. "Why do you want to talk about Valerie?" he asked.

"I want to write about the search for her fifteen years ago. It was the largest wilderness search in county history, and as a result of that search, Eagle Mountain Search and Rescue instituted a lot of new policies and adopted a more professional approach to their operations."

"You know she was never found," he said. "It's not exactly a feel-good story."

"No, but it's an enduring mystery."

He braced himself for her to say that people were always interested in mysteries. That was true, but when it was your own family tragedy at the center of the mystery, it was tough to think of it as entertaining. But she gave him a direct look, her blue eyes showing no sign of guile. "It doesn't hurt to bring the case to the public's attention again. You never know when someone might have seen the one thing that could help you find out what happened that day."

"Do you really think there's a person out there who knows something they've never talked about?" he asked. "I'm pretty sure the sheriff's department—not to mention my parents—talked to everyone they could find."

"There was another camper in the area that day. No one ever found and talked to him."

"How do you know about him?"

"One of the news stories from the paper's archives mentioned law enforcement was looking for the man."

"He was backpacking, like us. It's not like he could have smuggled my sister out in his pack or anything. The general consensus was that Valerie fell or had some other accident. It's pretty rugged country, and there are a lot of places a little kid could get lost."

She glanced at her notes. "I plan to meet with the sheriff, and search and rescue has agreed to let me review their logs and other information in the archives about the search. And I want to speak with your parents."

"Let me call them first."

"That would be great." She smiled, and he felt the impact of the expression. How could someone put so much warmth into a smile? "I'll wait until I hear from you before I contact them. But it would help a lot if you could tell me about that day. I'd like to know more about Valerie and what she was like, and what your family was like before that day."

"I was only ten when it happened."

"She was your twin. You must have memories of her."

"I do."

She leaned toward him, her voice gentle. "I'm not trying to cause you pain, opening up old wounds. But Valerie is at the center of the story. I want to try to show my readers how her loss affected not just her family but also this town. I have a quote from the newspaper stories at the time. One of the volunteer searchers said that before Valerie disappeared, everyone thought of the wilderness as safe—not without risk, but a haven from the kinds of crimes that happen in cities and towns. That sense of security was taken along with her."

"We don't know that her disappearance was a crime."

"No. But because her body was never found—not a single trace—the possibility remains that someone took her. It's every family's worst nightmare, isn't it?"

"Yeah." A nightmare. One from which they had never completely awakened.

Fifteen Years Ago

"COME ON, VINCE. Race me to that big red rock up ahead." Valerie turned around and walked backward along the trail, thumbs hooked in the straps of her blue backpack, her legs like two pale sticks between the frayed hem of her denim shorts and the folded cuffs of the striped knit socks she wore with her green leather hiking boots. She had had what their mom deemed a growth spurt that summer, and was now three inches taller than Vince and all angles. Except for the corkscrew curls that stuck out from the green bandanna she had tied around her head.

"I don't want to race," he said. He didn't even want to be on this trip, lugging a heavy pack up into the middle of nowhere instead of hanging out with his friends at Trevor Richardson's birthday party, which was going to be a pool party at the rec center in Junction. Some of the boys—including Vince—had been invited to spend the night, with sleeping bags in the Richardsons' basement rec room, where they planned to stay up all night eating junk food and watching horror movies.

But Vince's parents had put an end to that prospect, insisting Vince needed to come on this trip. "We've been planning it for weeks, and family comes first," his mother said when Vince had protested.

So here he was, with the straps of his backpack digging into his shoulders and Valerie doing her best to be the kid who was *soooo* happy to be here. Instead of sympathizing with her twin, she was purposely making him look bad.

"How can anybody be such a grumpy-pants when we're surrounded by all this gorgeousness?" Valerie turned to face forward again and raised her arms in the air like she was auditioning for *The Sound of Music* or something.

No one answered her. Instead, their dad said, "I think there's a good spot to camp up ahead, off to the left in the shelter of that dike." He pointed toward a gray rock wall that stood out from the rest of the more eroded mountainside. An amateur geologist, Dad liked to use these trips to talk about various rock formations and how they had come to be. Usually, Vince found this interesting, but how could that stuff—much of which he had heard before—compare to the lost prospect of swimming, pizza, and a sleepover with unlimited junk food and horror movies?

"Awesome!" Valerie raced toward the campsite, pack bouncing. Vince brought up the rear of the group. When he got there, Valerie had already scaled a flat-topped chunk of granite. "There's another camper over there!" She pointed straight ahead. "Looks like a guy with a blue dome tent."

"Come down and help set up camp," their mother said. She was already pulling the rain fly and a bag of stakes from her pack while their father unpacked the folded tent. They each carried their own sleeping bags and pads, and the food for the weekend was divided among them.

"I'll help with the tent," Valerie said.

"Vince can help with that," their father said. "Why don't

you see if you can find firewood? I thought I spotted some dead trees on the other side of the trail."

Valerie raced off to gather wood while Vince reluctantly helped his dad assemble the tent. "There will be other parties," his father said.

"Not like this one." Vince pounded a tent stake into the hard ground. "And there will be lots of other camping trips."

"Maybe. But you and your sister are growing up fast. In a few years you'll have jobs, then you'll be going away to college. It won't be as easy for the four of us to get away. These trips are important, though you may not realize how important until you're older."

"Trevor's party was important to me."

His dad paused in the act of feeding one of the collapsible tent poles through the channel in the top of the tent. "I can understand that. And maybe insisting you come with us wasn't the fairest decision, but it's the one I made. It's too late to go back, so you might as well try to make the best of it. Maybe we'll do something for your birthday to make up for it. I can't promise a pool party, but you could invite your friends to spend the night and watch movies."

"Really?"

Dad smiled. "I don't see why not."

Vince grinned. Wait until the guys heard about this! Then his elation faded. "What about Valerie?" He and his twin always celebrated together, usually with a joint party, featuring games and cake and ice cream.

"The two of you are old enough for separate celebrations, I think. I'll talk to your mom."

"Thanks!" By the time they had finished with the tent, he was feeling better. He helped spread the pads and sleeping bags inside, then emerged to find the light already fading, the air cooling. He retrieved a fleece pullover from his pack. "Find your sister and tell her to come back to camp," his mother said.

He crossed the road and hadn't gone far before he met Valerie staggering toward him, arms full of dead tree branches. She was dropping more than she was transporting, and he hurried to take half the load from her.

"I met our neighbor," she said when both loads were balanced.

"Who?"

"The man who's camped over there." She nodded up the road. "He was looking for firewood too, but he said I could have this and he would look somewhere else."

"What's his name?"

"He didn't say. He just smiled and left. He had a nice smile." Her dimple deepened at the recollection.

"You're not supposed to talk to strangers," Vince said.

"I didn't say anything. He did all the talking."

"That's hard to believe. You never shut up."

She hip-checked him. He did the same to her. "You are such a dork!" she said.

"You're the champion dork."

"I'm number one!" she shouted, and ran ahead of him.

They raced into camp. Mom smiled at them. "As soon as the fire is going, I'll start supper," she said.

"What are we having?" Valerie asked.

"Sausage spaghetti."

"And s'mores for dessert?" Valerie asked.

"Yes."

"Yay!" Valerie shouted.

"Yay!" Vince echoed.

They ate all the spaghetti and the s'mores, then lay back by the campfire and watched for shooting stars. Vince counted five of them streaking across the sky in the space of half an hour. Valerie nudged him. "Admit it, you're glad you came," she said.

"I wish I could have done both—the party and this."

"Yeah. That would have been fun. But I'm glad you're here."

He fell asleep there on the ground, and his father woke him to go into the tent, where he burrowed into his sleeping bag beside Valerie. She lay curled on her side, the rhythm of her deep breathing lulling him to sleep.

He woke early the next morning when she crawled over him on her way to the door. "What are you doing?" he whispered, then glanced toward their parents, who slept side by side a few inches away.

"I'm going to get wood and start a fire." Valerie pulled on one green boot, then the other, then ducked out the tent flap and zipped it up again.

He lay down again and must have fallen back asleep. Next thing he knew, his mother was shaking him. "Vince, have you seen your sister?"

"Huh?" He raised up on his elbows and looked around. Valerie and his dad were both gone from the tent, and his mother was dressed in tan hiking shorts and a blue fleece, her brown hair pulled back in a ponytail.

"Valerie isn't here. Do you know where she went?" Mom asked.

"She got up early and said she was going to get firewood." He sat up. Bright sunlight showed through the open tent flap. "What time is it?"

"It's after eight. When did she get up?"

"I don't know. Really early, I think." He had that impression, anyway.

"Get up and get dressed. We need to look for her."

When he crawled out of the tent, he noticed the firepit was empty and cold. "Valerie!" his mother called.

"Valerie!" His dad echoed from the other side of the dike.

Vince climbed onto the granite slab and shaded his eyes, searching for movement or a flash of color. His father joined him. "Do you see anything?" Dad asked.

"No. Yesterday, she said there was a man camped over here, but I don't see anyone."

"Come on. We need to spread out and look farther away."

They searched for an hour. Vince peered into canyons and climbed atop rocks, but there was no sign of Valerie. "I'm going to hike back to the car and go for the sheriff," his father said. "You stay with your mother and keep looking."

His mother pulled him close. Her eyes were red and swollen from crying. "Where could she have gone?" she asked. "Did she say where she was going?"

"No. She just said she was going to get some wood."

"How can she have just vanished?"

But she had. None of them would ever see her again.

Chapter Three

Tammy met with Sheriff Travis Walker on Monday morning. When she had first moved to Eagle Mountain, the handsome dark-haired sheriff was considered one of the most eligible bachelors in town. Now the married father of twins, he had a reputation for being an honest, hardworking lawman who had run unopposed in the last election. Not long after Tammy had started work at the newspaper, she had been attacked by a pair of men who had been preying on women in the area. She had escaped unharmed, and Travis had been gentle, but firm, in digging out all the information she could remember about her attackers.

As she waited in his office, she studied the photo of his smiling wife, a baby in each arm. It probably wasn't easy being married to a man who had to face his share of danger, but Lacey Walker looked happy. Tammy felt a pinch of jealousy as she stared at the photo. She wanted that kind of happiness—that settledness of having a mate who loved you and children who were part of you. So far, that had eluded her.

"Hello, Tammy." She turned as Travis entered the office. He settled behind the desk, the chair creaking as he sat back. "Sorry to keep you waiting."

"I haven't been here long."

"I had a copy of the Valerie Shepherd file made for you.

There's not a lot of information here." He handed a single file folder across the desk.

"I spoke with Vince Shepherd Friday," she said. "He told me the consensus was that Valerie must have fallen and either been killed instantly or so injured she wasn't able to cry for help."

"By all accounts, she was an active, adventurous little girl," Travis said. "There are a lot of steep drop-offs, deep canyons and unstable rock formations in the area."

"But if that was the case, don't you think someone would have found her? According to the accounts I've read, there were literally hundreds of people searching for her for weeks. And yet not one item of clothing or any part of her remains has been found."

He shrugged. "If she ended up deep in a canyon, or in a cave or rock crevice, her remains might never be discovered."

"What about the other camper who was in the area? A single man."

"I can only tell you what's in the file, since I wasn't part of the force then. The notes you'll find in there indicate that while Valerie mentioned seeing a man camping a short distance away from the Shepherd family, no one else in the family actually saw him, and no one else we talked to saw him either."

"Do you think she was making him up? Was she like that?"

"I don't know. I'm mentioning it as one possibility."

She opened the file folder and began flipping through the notes and reports inside, scanning each page. She stopped at one report. "This says a deputy spoke to a couple of hikers who saw a man with a backpack in the area. He was alone, and they never saw him again."

"He might be the man Valerie saw, or he might be someone else," Travis said. "The department put out an appeal asking anyone who had been in the area that day to come forward, but no one ever did."

She closed the file and looked at him again. "Were there ever any suspects?"

"None," Travis said.

"What about the family? Could one of them have done something to Valerie and hidden it from the others? I know it's horrible to think about, but it does happen."

"There are copies of interviews with each family member, as well as background information from neighbors and teachers who knew them. Everyone agreed that Valerie was a loved, well-cared-for child. The parents and her brother were devastated by her loss."

"Whenever I write stories like this, I always hope someone will come forward with new information," she said. "We usually run a box at the end of the article that asks anyone who might have information to contact the sheriff's department."

"I'd be happy to hear from anyone who could shed more light on what happened that day, but I think it's doubtful that will happen."

"Probably not. Of course, the main point of the article is to highlight the efforts of search and rescue that day. Can I get a quote from you about that?"

"My understanding is that prior to Valerie's disappearance, the group was a loose-knit band of volunteers without the formal structure they have today. They worked with local law enforcement, but they weren't under the direction of the sheriff's department, as they are today. Today Eagle Mountain Search and Rescue is a professional, highly trained organization I would consider one of the best in the mountain west."

She scribbled the quote in her notebook. "That's great," she said. "Exactly what I'm looking for."

He flashed one of his rare smiles. "I'm glad I could help."

She left the sheriff's department and was walking back to the newspaper office when a voice hailed her. She turned and was surprised to see her younger brother, Mitch, striding toward her. Mitch had inherited their father's darker, straighter hair, which he wore long and pulled back in a ponytail. Dressed in fashionably cut jeans and a loose linen shirt, he looked ready to make a deal on Wall Street or—a more likely scenario—sell a luxurious vacation home to that Wall Street denizen.

"How's the real estate business?" she asked as Mitch drew even with her.

"I just came from a showing I hope will result in a sale of a ranch over near the county line," he said. "Now I have time to kill and thought I'd see if you wanted to grab lunch."

"I do if you're buying," she said. She nudged him with her elbow. "Seeing as you're about to earn a big commission and everything."

"It's not a done deal yet," he said. "But I can buy my sister lunch." He hugged her briefly. "How are you doing?"

"I'm doing okay."

"Not better than okay? Are you still upset about Darrell?"

"No, I am not upset about Darrell." Not anymore. Breaking things off with him had been the right decision, she knew. He wasn't interested in ever settling down and she was ready to look for something long term. "Ending things between us was sad," she said. "But I know it was the right thing to do."

"You'll find someone else," he said. "Maybe a handsome, wealthy, single, straight man looking to make his home in Eagle Mountain will walk into my office this afternoon and I'll introduce him to you."

"Please do," she said, and laughed.

"Where should we have lunch?" he asked.

"Let me drop this off at my office, then you can pick," she said, holding up the file folder.

He gestured at the file. "Something you're working on?"

"I'm writing about the search fifteen years ago for a little girl who went missing."

"How old was this girl?"

"Ten."

The lines across his forehead deepened. "Why are you writing about something that happened that long ago?"

She explained her planned series of articles focusing on Eagle Mountain Search and Rescue.

"And she was ten, huh?"

"Yeah, I know." The same age as their older brother, Adam, when he had been killed by a speeding car. "I interviewed the girl's twin brother Friday. When he talked about feeling lost after she was gone, I knew exactly what he was going through." She had been nine when Adam was killed, Mitch seven. Young enough to not fully comprehend how someone could suddenly be gone. Old enough to see the way their family changed forever on that day.

"Did you tell him about Adam?" Mitch asked.

"No. It's not something I talk about with anyone but you." Her mother, the only parent left now, had long ago stopped talking about her eldest son, the memories too painful.

"Yeah, me either."

She left the file on her desk; then she and Mitch walked over two blocks to the edge of the park and a food truck that sold tacos and other Mexican street food. She and Mitch had just settled at a picnic table with their purchases when Vince and two other men in the khaki uniform shirts of Eagle

Mountain Road and Bridge took their place in line. "Hey, Tammy," Vince said.

"Hi, Vince. How are you?"

"Can't complain." Then he was called to place his order, and he turned away.

"Who is that?" Mitch asked.

"Vince Shepherd. Valerie's brother."

"Is he single?"

"Why? Are you interested?"

He made a face. "I was thinking for you."

It was her turn to scowl at him.

"I'm just saying," he said. "The two of you seem to get along well."

She laughed. "Saying hello to each other doesn't tell you anything about how we'd get along."

He held up both hands in a defensive gesture. "Don't blame me for wanting you to be happy."

"I am happy," she said. Maybe not the level of happiness she craved, but life wasn't all bliss and she didn't expect it to be. She touched her brother's wrist. "I'm fine, Mitch. You don't have to worry about me."

"Just don't go stirring up trouble with this article."

"Oh, please. There's nothing about this article that could cause me trouble. I'm not an investigative reporter digging up dirt in a big city." Maybe in another life, she would have chosen a more exciting career, but being the sole reporter at a small-town paper suited her. It was comfortable and safe, and that's what she craved—most of the time, at least.

"I DIDN'T KNOW you knew Tammy Patterson," Vince's co-worker, Cavin, said when the three of them were seated at a table a short distance from where Tammy and her friend were eating.

"We've met." Vince poured salsa onto his tacos.

"I heard she split up with the guy she was dating," the third man at the table, Sandor, said.

Vince stared at him. "How do you know these things?"

"My wife works at the salon where Tammy gets her hair cut. She knows everything there is to know about half the female population in town. And then she comes home and tells me everything."

"The scary thing is, you remember it," Cavin said.

Sandor shrugged. "People are interesting."

"If you say so." Vince bit into his taco. He glanced over at Tammy. She was pretty, in a friendly, down-to-earth kind of way. All those soft curls. She was laughing with the guy she was with.

Cavin nudged him. "Caught you looking," he said.

Vince focused on his food once more. "She and that guy look pretty cozy, so I'd say she isn't available," he said.

"That's her brother," Sandor said. "He's a real estate agent over at Brown Realty. He helped us find the house we're in."

Vince couldn't help himself—he had to look at the pair again. Maybe a family resemblance was there. Tammy rested a hand on the man's forearm and smiled into his eyes. He felt a pang. What would it be like to have a lunch with a grown-up Valerie like that? To have someone besides your parents who had known you your whole life, who had seen life from a similar perspective and had the same frame of reference? He would never know.

Cavin shifted the conversation to a discussion of parts he needed to order for one of the county graders, and Vince turned his back on Tammy and her brother. Maybe he wasn't cut out for relationships. He didn't like getting too close to people. That was okay. Everybody was different, and he was happy enough. Most of the time.

"As we say goodbye to our friend Paul, it is with great sadness, as well as gratitude for having him in our lives. Though his physical body is gone from us, his memory endures, and we will hold him in our hearts forever." The black-suited man from the funeral home who had agreed to lead this graveside burial looked across the open grave at the trio of mourners. "Go in peace," he said. "And I'm sorry for your loss."

"Thank you." Valerie choked out the words, then cleared her throat, pulling herself together. Paul never liked it when she cried. It was the one thing she did that ever made him angry. She turned away, not wanting to see them shovel dirt onto the coffin.

"It's hard to believe he's gone."

She glanced at the speaker—Bill, who had played on the local softball team with Paul. "I guess so," she said. Though after staring at his dead body, slumped in his favorite chair in front of the TV, she hadn't any doubts that he had died. An asthma attack, the coroner had said.

"I mean, he was so young," Bill continued. "Only forty-five."

Thirty-nine, she silently corrected. But he told everyone he was older because of her. She hadn't realized herself until she had found papers with his real age on them one day when she was sixteen. It made sense, though. No one would have believed he was her father if they knew he was only fourteen years older. Not that it was anyone's business.

"I know there's not any formal wake or anything, but do you want to get coffee or something?"

She stopped walking. So did Bill. He shoved his hands in the pockets of his baggy suit and hunched his shoulders the way tall people sometimes did, as if trying to look smaller. He was thin and bony, and already losing his hair despite the fact that he was still in his twenties. He wasn't bad looking, but his cloying infatuation with her was grating. "No thank you," she said. "I don't feel like company."

"Well, sure. Of course." He took a step back. "Maybe another time."

She walked alone to her car and drove back to the house that had been home the past fifteen years, in a drab suburb of Omaha, Nebraska. She had been happy here while Paul was alive. Happy enough. Happy as a person could be who had been abandoned by the people who were supposed to take care of her. As Paul had often reminded her, she was lucky he had come along when he did, to look after her.

But now Paul was gone. She had no one.

She was alone now. Free to do whatever she wanted. Paul had left her a little money—several thousand in cash he kept in the safe in his bedroom closet, as well as the house and ample funds in the bank accounts they shared. She would take that money and spend some time making things right.

Chapter Four

Monday night, Vince called his parents. He had been putting the conversation off since he had talked to Tammy on Friday, but it was time he let them know. Though they had moved to Junction several years before, they still subscribed to the *Eagle Mountain Examiner*, and he didn't want them surprised by Tammy's request for an interview. Besides, she was waiting on him before she could finish the article.

His father answered the phone and put the call on Speaker right away. "Hello, Vince," he said. "Your mother is right here. How are you doing?"

"I'm okay, Dad. How are you and Mom?"

"We're fine," his mom answered. "A little tired. We played golf today—a full eighteen holes. With Barb and Ray Ferngil. Do you remember them? Ray used to work with your dad."

Vince had no idea who they were talking about. "You had beautiful weather for a game," he said.

"We did," his dad said. "I like living near a good course."

"Did you just call to chat, or did you need something?" his mom asked. "Not that we don't love to hear from you, but you don't usually call on a Monday night."

"A reporter here in Eagle Mountain is doing a series of articles on the local search and rescue organization," he said.

"One of the articles is going to be about the search for Valerie. I just wanted to warn you so it didn't come as a shock."

"Oh." One short, sad exhalation from his mom that made his chest tighten. He hoped she wasn't going to start crying. She hadn't done that in a long time, but it always unsettled him.

"Did this reporter talk to you about it?" his dad asked. "Is that how you know?"

"Yeah. She interviewed me. I think it's going to be a good story. Apparently, the search for Valerie was a catalyst that transformed the rescue group into a professional organization."

"Well, good. Good." He could picture his dad nodding in that thoughtful way he had—lips pursed, brow furrowed.

"She wants to talk to you and Mom too."

"Well…" Now he pictured his father looking at his mother, gauging her reaction to the request.

"Of course we'll talk to her," his mom said. "Maybe someone will come forward who remembers something about that day that got overlooked. Or the article will inspire people to look for her while they're hiking in that area."

"Maybe so, Mom. Though after such a long time, I don't think we can hope for much."

"You never know. Maybe…maybe Valerie will see the article and get in touch."

He winced. His parents—especially his mother—had never given up hope that Valerie hadn't died that day but that she had been taken, perhaps by the mysterious camper no one had ever identified. "I don't know about that, Mom," he said.

"I know you think I'm foolish, but it's not such a far-fetched idea. There have been other missing children who were discovered as adults. And I still say if Valerie had died that day, someone would have found her. You may not remember, but they literally had people spaced two feet apart in long lines, searching every inch of the area around our campsite for miles. How could they have not found her if she was still there?"

"I didn't mean to upset you," Vince said. "I just wanted you to know."

"We appreciate that," his dad said. Gone was the cheerfulness with which he had started the call. Now he sounded tired. Old.

"I'll let you know if I hear anything else," Vince said. "I'd better go now."

"Goodbye, son." This from his dad. In the background, he heard a sound he thought might have been his mother, crying.

He ended the call and leaned against the sofa, head back, eyes closed. For years, his mom had sworn that if Valerie was dead, she would know it. "She's my daughter," she said. "That's a bond that doesn't break."

Once, years ago, she had pressed Vince to admit that he still felt his sister was alive too. "She's your twin," Mom said. "You're halves of the same whole."

"We're not identical twins, Mom."

"Oh, you know what I mean."

"I'm sorry, Mom, I don't."

"You don't feel Valerie is still alive somewhere?"

"I don't know, Mom."

Her face crumpled, but she pulled herself together. "Do you feel like she's gone, then?" she asked.

"I don't know, Mom."

When he thought of his sister, he didn't feel anything. Just…empty. Not a wrenching loss or a sense that she was just away for a while. There was a void where his sister was supposed to be, and he didn't expect anything would ever fill it.

AT THE THURSDAY-evening meeting of Eagle Mountain Search and Rescue volunteers. Vince settled on one end of the sofa in the hangar-like building that served as search and rescue headquarters, next to newlyweds Jake and Hannah Gwynn. When he wasn't volunteering with SAR, Jake was a deputy with the Rayford County Sheriff's Department, which put him on the scene for many of the accidents SAR responded to. After seeing the volunteers in action, he had decided to join their ranks. And it had been one way to guarantee he would see more of Hannah.

"All right, everyone. Let's go ahead and get started." Danny, clipboard in hand, walked to the front of the room, and conversation among the volunteers died down. "First up, I want to introduce our newest volunteer, Bethany Ames."

A slender young woman with a mass of dark curls stood and waved. She had a heart-shaped face and an upturned nose, and a dimple in her cheek when she smiled. "Bethany is new to the area and works at Peak Jeep and Snowmobile Rentals," Danny continued. "Everyone, introduce yourselves later." Bethany sat, and Danny consulted his clipboard again. "Next, most of you already know that this summer marks the twenty-fifth anniversary of the founding of Eagle Mountain Search and Rescue."

"Happy birthday to us!" Ryan Welch called out while several others responded with whistles or clapping.

"Will there be a cake?" someone else asked.

"Cake is always welcome," Danny agreed. "We'll see what we can do. In the meantime, the *Eagle Mountain Examiner* is planning a series of articles about the organization, focusing on several of our missions over the years, as well as sharing how the group has grown and changed."

Murmurs of approval greeted this news.

"The first article is going to run next week. Most of you

know Tammy Patterson, the paper's reporter. She's starting the series with a feature about the search for Valerie Shepherd fifteen years ago."

A number of people turned to look at Vince. "Are you okay with this?" Jake asked.

"I already spoke with Tammy," Vince said. "It's fine."

"Valerie was never found," Tony Meisner, the volunteer who had been with the group longest—over twenty years—said. "Why start with that mission?"

"Because that search—and the failure of anyone to find Valerie—changed the way the group organized and trained," Danny said. "After that, we formally operated under the direction of the sheriff, we required more training, restructured the command system with new roles, and sought accreditation with the Colorado Search and Rescue Association."

Tony sat back. "Okay, that makes sense. Still seems a bummer to start with such a sad case." He looked over at the sofa. "No offense, Vince. I always felt bad we didn't find your sister."

"It's okay," Vince said. "I know everyone tried their best." He didn't remember that much about the actual search for Valerie. His parents had kept him home, perhaps fearful that he might wander off and come to harm. But he had seen the appeals for people to help with the search, and photographs in the paper showing lines of volunteers marching across the area where they had camped.

"This series is going to be great publicity for the group," Danny said. "We want to take advantage of that by stepping up our fundraising."

Groans rose up around the room. "I know, I know," Danny said. "Nobody likes begging for money. But the work we do is expensive—equipment constantly needs replacing and supplies replenishing. Training costs money, and then there are the everyday expenses, like gas for vehicles and utility bills for this building and the occasional meal to keep you people from resigning. We rely on donations for the bulk of our funds."

"I guess when people read this article and think about how great and wonderful we are, we might as well be there with our hands out," Ryan said.

Many in the group laughed. Danny smiled. "The paper has agreed to print a coupon people can use to mail in a donation, as well as information about how they can donate online. We're also going to have our usual booth at the community Fourth of July celebration," he said. He held up the clipboard. "I've got the sign-up sheet here. We've also been asked to participate in something the city is calling First Responders Fun Fair."

"What is that?" Sheri asked.

"The Elks Club is hosting their usual carnival games, but this time they're asking fire, sheriff's, EMS and SAR personnel to man the various games, with all the proceeds from ticket sales split among the four groups. Last year they took in almost five thousand dollars in proceeds, so it's a significant addition to our coffers."

"Sure, we can do that," Eldon Ramsey said.

"I have a sign-up sheet for the carnival as well. Everyone needs to come up and choose your time slots." He set the clipboard aside. "No training tonight, but we do need to pull out and inspect all the climbing gear and reorganize and replenish first aid supplies. Sheri and Tony are in charge of the climbing gear, while Hannah and I will oversee the first aid supplies. We each need people to help, so spread out and let's get to work."

Vince was trying to decide who to work with when Bethany approached. "Hi," she said. "Have you been with search and rescue long?"

"About six months," he said. "So I'm still a rookie too."

"It's a little intimidating being around so many experienced volunteers." She scanned the room. "I don't have any special skills, but Danny said I didn't need them, just a willingness to work and follow direction."

"You'll do fine," Vince said. "Everyone here pitches in to help the newbies learn the ropes."

Her expression sobered. "I was sorry to hear about your sister."

"Um, thanks." She was looking at him with those big, dark eyes, her expression a familiar one—mixed curiosity and pity. He never knew how to respond to that, so he was relieved when Tony approached. "Come help with the climbing gear," he said. He glanced at Bethany. "I know Hannah could use another hand with the medical supplies."

"Sure. Thanks." Bethany touched his arm. "It was nice talking with you, Vince," she said, and hurried away.

Vince and Tony moved to the closet that held the ropes and hardware used in climbing. The steep canyons and high peaks of the terrain around Eagle Mountain meant that many of their rescue operations involved climbing or rappelling, and a significant part of volunteer training focused on the skills needed for these activities. Sheri and Tony began laying out ropes, and she explained how to inspect the colored braided strands for damage and excessive wear.

Vince accepted a coil of rope from Tony. He realized the veteran was the only one here tonight who'd been part of the search when Valerie disappeared. "Did you help look for my sister?" he asked.

"I did." The lines around his blue eyes deepened. Lean and muscular, Tony had the weathered complexion of a man who spent a lot of time outdoors, his neat beard and blond hair beginning to show streaks of gray. "We went out every day for a week."

"What was that like?" Vince asked. "I mean, what about it led to so many changes for the group?"

Tony considered the question for a long moment, then said, "It wasn't that we were disorganized, but we hadn't had any formal training. We knew some basic principles, but the training we get nowadays teaches us about the psychology of searches. People who are lost have patterns of behavior. Most people tend to stick to trails or roads, even animal trails. In the mountains, they tend to move up, to try to get a better view of terrain. They may believe no one is looking for them and they have to walk out of a situation to be found, which may lead them to keep moving, even if they're disoriented and have no idea where they are. Today we use mapping techniques and even mathematical formulas to determine the most likely area a person will be located, and focus the search on these areas first. We didn't have any of that kind of data fifteen years ago—we just tried to search as wide an area as possible, with no precision."

"Does it seem odd to you that no trace of her was ever discovered?" Vince asked. "Not a piece of clothing or a bone or anything?"

"One thing I know now that I didn't know then was that children will sometimes hide from searchers or refuse to answer when people, even family members, call for them," he said. "They're afraid of getting into trouble. We might have walked right by your sister and not known she was there if she didn't respond to our calls. Then too, there's a lot of country up there, much of it rough and pretty inaccessible. Most people who die in the back country are found eventually, but not everyone. I'm sorry."

"We always wondered if she was taken."

"That happens too," Tony said. "But who took her? There was no one else up there."

"Valerie said there was a man camped near us. None of us ever saw him, but we didn't look. And she wasn't one to make things up."

"Then maybe that's what happened. If it is, I'm sorry about that too."

Vince knew the statistics. Children who were taken were almost always killed unless they were kidnapped by a relative, and he was pretty sure that hadn't happened to Valerie. He didn't like to think of his sister ending up that way, any more than he wanted to believe she had fallen into a crevice in the mountains and been killed. He had long believed she had died, but he wanted to know how. Wasn't that human nature—to not like unanswered questions?

IN THE FOUR years Tammy had been reporting for the *Eagle Mountain Examiner*, she had written feel-good pieces about local citizens; straightforward accounts of town council and school board meetings; reports of burglaries, fires and murder. She had even written a first-person report of her own escape from a pair of serial killers who had terrorized the area one winter. While some of these stories had been tougher to write than others, none had affected her as much as her recounting of the disappearance of Valerie Shepherd.

More than one volunteer had teared up as they spoke of the search for the little girl. "She used to come into my store with her mom," said the owner of the local meat market. "Such a grin on her face. She was an impish kind of kid—always up to something. Her twin brother was quieter, following her lead. We couldn't believe she would just vanish the way she did."

"It hit me hard," another volunteer admitted. "I wouldn't let my own kids out of my sight for a long time after that. To think of anything like that happening here, where we always felt safe. It was hard to believe things could change that suddenly—one minute she was there, the next she was gone."

But Tammy knew how suddenly life could change. The day Adam had been killed, the three of them—Adam, Mitch and her—had been playing in the front yard, kicking a soccer ball back and forth, when the ball had rolled into the street. "I'll get it!" Adam called, and ran after it.

He didn't see the car race around the curve. And the driver didn't see Adam until it was too late. One minute he had been there with them, laughing and playing. The next moment he was gone. A hole was torn in their family that could never be repaired. They had done their best to heal, but they all carried the wound inside them.

She had seen the same kind of damage in Vince Shepherd when she had interviewed him. He knew what it was like to walk through life with an empty space in your heart or your soul that could never be filled. Tammy coped by avoiding thinking about Adam and what had happened that day. But talking to Vince and to the volunteer searchers had forced her to feel all those feelings again—grief and anger and confusion. How could something like that happen? How could a person who was practically part of you suddenly not be there?

She had wanted to ask Vince if he was like her—if he coped with the loss by avoiding thinking about it. She had apologized for bringing him and his family any pain, but was an apology enough?

That was why she turned up outside Vince's condo at eight thirty on a Wednesday night, a fresh copy of the latest issue of the *Examiner* in her hand. She rang the bell to his unit and shifted from foot to foot, jittery with nerves. What if he hated what she had written?

Footsteps sounded on the other side of the door, and then Vince stood on the threshold, a wary expression on his handsome face. His hair was damp, curling around his ears. The T-shirt that clung to his chest and abs was damp too, as if he had pulled it on hastily, along with the jeans. His feet were bare. "I didn't mean to disturb you," she blurted, feeling her face heat. "I just wanted to give you this." She thrust the paper at him. "Everyone else will see it in the morning, but I wanted you to read it first."

He unfolded the paper and scanned the headlines, stopping at the story that filled the front page below the fold. "'Search for Missing Girl Shaped EMSAR Future.'"

Tammy bit her lower lip and forced herself to remain still as he read. She had rewritten the lede so many times she had memorized it. *When ten-year-old Valerie Shepherd vanished from the mountains above Galloway Basin on a sunny summer Saturday, she changed the family who loved her forever. But she also changed the community of Eagle Mountain. And her disappearance spurred the transformation of Eagle Mountain Search and Rescue from a group of dedicated amateurs to the highly trained professional-quality organization they are today.*

Vince glanced up from the paper. He didn't look upset, which was a relief. "Come on in," he said, and took a step back.

"Okay. Sure." She moved past him, the scent of his soap—something herbal—distracting her, not to mention the realization that mere inches separated her from his seriously ripped body. How had she not noticed this the other night? He hadn't been wearing a clinging, wet T-shirt, but still, how had she missed those shoulders?

She pushed the thought away and moved into a small living room furnished with a sofa, matching chair, coffee table and a large wall-mounted television. He slipped past her, picked up the remote and switched off the TV. "Have a seat," he said.

She settled on one end of the sofa. He took the other, the newspaper spread out on his lap. "Thanks for bringing this by," he said.

"I figured people might mention the article to you, and you'd want to know what's in it."

He nodded and looked down, reading again. She gripped both knees and pretended to study the room, but she was almost entirely focused on Vince, attuned to any reaction he might have to her words.

He was a fast reader. Or maybe he was skimming. Not many seconds passed before he looked up again. "It's good," he said. "All the stuff about search and rescue is interesting. I didn't realize all the emphasis on training was relatively new."

"Part of that is because there's a lot more training courses available now."

He glanced back down at the paper. "I didn't know so many people still think about Valerie. I always figured my mom and dad and me were the only ones who remembered her."

"I didn't have to remind anyone about what happened," Tammy said. "As soon as I said her name, they remembered. And everyone asked if I knew anything more about what happened to her."

"I guess no one came up with any new information? I mean, the article doesn't mention anything."

"There's nothing new. I'm sorry."

"I guess it would be surprising to think anything else would come to light after all this time."

"Will you share that with your parents?" She tapped the

paper. "I should have brought a copy for them too. I wasn't thinking."

"It's okay. They have a subscription. They're looking forward to the article. Dad said they enjoyed talking to you."

"I enjoyed talking with them." Though, in some ways, it had been uncomfortably like talking with her own mother—the familiar sad and wistful expressions, along with the way they second-guessed every action that day. If they had done this instead of that, maybe they could have prevented what had happened.

"My dad said you were empathetic. I guess that's an important quality for a writer."

She looked away, then forced her gaze back to him. No reason not to tell him. "I had a brother, Adam. He died when he was ten. I was nine. We were playing in the front yard of our house—me and Adam and our brother, Mitch—and our soccer ball rolled into the street. Adam ran after it and was hit by a car."

"Then you know what it's like," he said. "Everything is fine, and the next second, nothing will ever be the same again."

"Yeah." The lump in her throat startled and embarrassed her. After all this time, she didn't cry about Adam. What good would that do? But her eyes stung and her chest tightened. She clenched her fists, digging her nails into her palms. "What happened to Adam was terrible," she said. "But at least we know what happened to him." There was a grave her mother visited, though Tammy never did. The Shepherds didn't even have that.

"That was your brother with you at lunch the other day, right?" Vince asked.

"Yes. Mitch."

"It's nice that he's here in town. I always wondered if it

would have been a little easier if I had had a sibling. Someone else for my parents to focus on. Someone else who had the same story I did."

"It was comforting having Mitch, especially right after Adam died, when my parents were struggling. He and I made sure to look after each other."

"I would have liked that, but I got used to being on my own. And my folks pulled themselves together after a while."

"They seem like great people."

"What about your parents?" he asked. "Do they live near here?"

"My dad died five years ago. But my mom is here. She and I share a house, actually."

"I don't think I could live with my parents again."

"My mom is a pretty good roommate."

Silence. He was looking down at the newspaper again, and she started to feel awkward. She stood. "I won't keep you. I just wanted to drop that off."

He set aside the paper and rose also. "Thanks."

He followed her to the door. When he had first invited her inside, hope had flickered that maybe they could connect on another level. As friends. Maybe even potential dates. Not that she was eager to rush into anything, but Vince was single, good-looking and close to her age. She couldn't deny a certain attraction, and while lost siblings maybe wasn't the most solid foundation on which to build a relationship, it did give them something in common.

Now all she wanted to do was get out of his condo. Everything felt too awkward and forced. She shouldn't have told him about Adam. It was too personal. Too close to home. She hoped he hadn't thought she was using her tragedy to get close to him. The idea made her queasy. "Good night," she said, and reached for the doorknob.

He put his hand over hers. He had big hands, and calluses on his fingers, the roughness registering against her skin, making her hyperaware of his physical presence. He wasn't an overly large man, but he was muscular and fit—so *male*. She would never write that in an article. The only reason she was even thinking it now was because he had her stirred up and confused. He looked into her eyes, and though she didn't move, she felt knocked off-balance. Such an intense look. Staggering. "Thanks for telling me about Adam," he said.

"I don't talk about him much," she said. "But I thought you'd understand."

"Yeah, I do." His gaze flickered to her lips, and she wondered if he was thinking about kissing her. Entirely inappropriate, and yet she fought to keep from leaning toward him, inviting his touch. *Okaaay.* She needed to get a grip.

"Good night," she said again. "I'll, uh, see you around."

She did turn the doorknob then, and he moved his hand away and stepped back. "Good night."

She managed to walk all the way to her car without breaking into a run or melting into a puddle. In her car, she sat and took deep breaths. What the heck had just happened in there? She had gone to Vince's condo to give him a copy of the newspaper, not to bare her soul or fall madly in lust. If he had felt even half of what she had, he was probably thinking she was the most unprofessional reporter he had ever met. Or worse, did he think she was chasing after him? She closed her eyes and rested her forehead against the steering wheel. Please, no, not that. She was not desperate, and she wanted nothing to do with a man who thought she was.

As for telling him about Adam, that hadn't been a bid for sympathy. She had wanted him to know she sympathized with that special brand of grief they shared. She was just being friendly, but too many times that kind of thing got misinterpreted. It had happened to her before. Once, when an intern at the paper arrived in town after a long day of travel, clearly exhausted and famished, she had invited him to dinner at her place. He had misinterpreted this as an attempt at seduction, which had embarrassed them both and made for an awkward six months as they worked side by side. Vince's father was right—she was an empathetic person. Too empathetic.

She straightened and started the car. Maybe she had embarrassed herself again tonight, but she would get over it. She had survived worse—what was one more injury to her dignity?

Chapter Five

All day Thursday, people stopped Vince to comment on the article in that day's paper. People expressed sympathy over the loss of his sister. Many wanted to hear Vince's take on what had happened that day, or hoped to glean details that hadn't been revealed in the article. "I never knew you had a sister," Sandor said as he and Vince made repairs to a guardrail that afternoon.

"It's not something I talk about." Vince shoved on the guardrail support to bring it into line. "Tighten that bolt there."

Sandor began tightening the bolt. "I wonder what happened to her. I mean, you think after all this time, they would have found something."

"You'd think. Okay, shove rocks up against this post to keep it upright. Then we'll pack the dirt down around it."

"I wonder if it was, like, aliens or something."

Vince stared. "Aliens."

"Yeah. I mean, what if she was abducted by aliens?"

"I don't believe in aliens."

Sandor frowned. "You don't? But there are a lot of stories…"

Vince shook his head. "Finish setting that post. I'm going to check the other side of the bridge."

No one else mentioned aliens, but several felt compelled

to share their theories, most involving kidnapping, or maybe, they said, Valerie had run away. Vince listened to them all, then found somewhere else he needed to be. It wasn't as if he hadn't already thought of all these things over the years— except the aliens. But without proof, he would never know what happened to his sister.

He arrived at his condo a little after five, ready to take a shower, have dinner and a drink, and binge TV. He was walking up to his door when a neighbor called out to him. He braced himself for sympathy or speculation as he waited for Tasha Brueger to reach him. "Hi, Vince," she said. "I just wanted to tell you there was a young woman here about an hour ago. She was asking about you."

"Who was she?"

"She didn't tell me her name. She just stopped me and asked if I knew when you'd be home. She was standing here at your front door. I guess she'd been ringing the bell and not getting an answer. I told her you usually got home a little after five."

He couldn't imagine who would be looking for him. Another reporter, maybe? "What did she look like?"

Tasha—who was a foot shorter than Vince's six feet and had to tilt her head back to look up at him—tugged on one long brown curl and pursed her lips, deep dimples forming on either side of her round cheeks. "She was just sort of average, you know? Dark hair, pulled back in a ponytail. Not too tall, not too short. Not fat or skinny. She wore sunglasses. I had to go pick Sammy up from practice, so we didn't talk long."

"Thanks." He turned back to his door, and Tasha hurried away. Could the woman looking for him have been Tammy Patterson? The description didn't really fit her, and if Tammy wanted to talk to him, why not call or text?

He let himself in and dropped his backpack by the door.

He wasn't sure if Tammy would ever want to see him again. Last night had ended awkwardly between them. That was all on him—he'd been caught so off guard by the intensity of his attraction to her that he had frozen. He considered himself a pro at keeping things casual when it came to women. His default setting for relationships might be summed up as "don't bother getting too close." But Tammy, with her warm smile and earnest expression—as well as the revelation about her brother's death—had cut through his carefully manufactured defenses with breathtaking ease. He didn't have to explain his feelings to her because she had experienced them herself.

Whether it was that understanding or her soft curves and cloud of blond curls, he had been bowled over by the desire to touch her. To kiss her. To discover what it would be like to be close to her. He thought she might be feeling a little of the same, but he couldn't be sure. If he had actually done any of the things his mind insisted on picturing, she might have slugged him. He knew plenty of women, but he couldn't say he knew *about* them. Would things be different if he had a sister to ask?

He shed his clothing as he walked down the hall and hit the shower. He closed his eyes and let the hot water beat down and willed himself not to think about anything for just a few minutes.

Half an hour later, he was in the kitchen, staring into the open refrigerator and trying to decide what to make for dinner, when his phone rang. It was a local number, so he answered. "Hi, Vince. It's Tammy." She sounded out of breath. Anxious.

"Hey. What's up?" Did he sound cool or just not too bright?

"Would it be okay if I came by your place for a few minutes? I have something I need to show you."

"Is everything okay? You sound upset." Or at least, less

than thrilled by the prospect of yet another awkward visit with him.

"I'm just…confused. Anyway, I think you need to see this."

"What is it?"

"I'd rather show you than talk about it."

"Okay. Sure. Come on by."

"I'll be right over."

He ended the call and closed the refrigerator, then leaned back against it, no longer hungry. Tammy had sounded rattled. He hadn't known her long, but she had struck him as a calm person. Someone who didn't panic easily.

He rubbed his jaw, and the scratch of whiskers made him wonder if he should shave. Would she think he was trying too hard?

He didn't have much time to wonder. Five minutes later, his doorbell rang. He opened it to Tammy. She was a little pale and a lot agitated. "Sorry to bother you again," she said as she rushed past him into the condo.

"No problem. Did you stop by earlier, before I got home?"

"What? No. No, I just left the office."

"Okay. What is it you need me to see?"

She looked around the room. "Can we sit down?" Without waiting for an answer, she started for the sofa.

"Do you want a drink or something?" he asked.

"Not now. Maybe after." She sat, then took an envelope from her purse and set the purse on the floor beside her. "Someone put this through the mail slot beside the door of the newspaper office this afternoon," she said, and tapped the envelope. "No one even uses that slot anymore—it's a relic from when the building was occupied by the electric company and people used the slot to leave their payments. But every once in a while we get a Letter to the Editor dropped off that way. When I came in about five o'clock and saw the envelope, that's what I thought this was. A complaint or something like that."

He sat beside her, angled toward her, their knees almost touching. "Whatever it is has you upset," he said. "Is it a threat or something?"

She thrust the letter toward him. "Read it," she said.

He took the envelope. It was a blank, white business-sized envelope, unsealed. He opened it and slid out a single sheet of white paper. The message on it was typewritten.

Nice article about the search for Valerie Shepherd. But you got a few things wrong about that day. More than a few things, actually. I don't blame you. You were sold a bunch of lies. I think people lie more than they tell the truth, especially when the lies make them look better. Maybe one day we'll meet and I'll tell you what really happened.

He scanned the brief message. This was what had Tammy so upset? This rambling from a person who couldn't possibly know what had happened? He glanced up from the sheet. "It's just someone babbling about lies," he said.

"Look at the bottom of the page," she said. "At the signature."

He let his gaze travel to the bottom of the sheet of paper, to a cursive scrawl in black ink. The hair on the back of his neck rose as he stared, and he had trouble breathing. No. He was letting his imagination run away from him. It didn't really say what he thought it said.

"It's signed *V*," Tammy said. "*V* for *Valerie*?"

"IT CAN'T BE VALERIE." Vince looked and sounded calmer than Tammy felt. She wasn't one to overreact, but those chilling

words about lies—and the single *V* at the bottom—had com-
bined to set her heart racing and her adrenaline flooding.
She had been alone in the newspaper office, with no one to
offer a different perspective, so she had called the one person she was sure would know the truth. Except, now that she
was here, she felt more foolish than frightened.

Vince dropped his gaze to the letter again, his eyes track-
ing the words across the page. Then he set the sheet of paper
aside on the coffee table in front of them. "No one lied that
day," he said. "At least, my parents didn't lie, and I didn't."

"Maybe the letter writer means someone else." Tammy
wet her dry lips and glanced at the letter as if it was a spi-
der she needed to keep an eye on in case it came any closer.
"Maybe there's someone who saw what happened to Valerie
and never spoke up."

"Then why not come forward and tell us what happened?"
His voice rose on the last words, anger edging out the calm
she suspected must have been an act. Of course he was upset.
Having someone impersonate his sister must have been a
horrible jolt.

"I'm sorry," she said. "I should have realized it was a fake.
I didn't mean to upset you."

"It's okay." He blew out a breath. "You didn't expect this,
but I should have. Every time any new publicity about Valerie's disappearance comes out, people like that come out of
nowhere." He nodded at the letter. "I don't know if they're
mentally ill or running a scam, or maybe both. I can't tell
you how many times my parents have dealt with this kind
of thing."

"How horrible for you all."

"It was. For months after she first went missing, they
would get calls from people who promised to find Valerie—
for a price. So-called psychics and private detectives. My

parents spent a lot of money paying off various people. They wanted so badly to believe it was Valerie that they lost all common sense. I'm betting this is more of the same."

"That makes me sick," she said. "What is wrong with people?"

"You're a reporter and you ask that?"

She let out a shaky laugh. "I guess I don't let people like that take up any more headspace than necessary." She glanced at the letter again. "Should I throw it away?"

"File it. Just in case this person decides to cause trouble." His expression grew troubled again. "I wonder if they were trying to shake me down too."

"What do you mean?"

"When I got home today, my neighbor told me a woman had stopped by looking for me. I thought it might have been you, but you said you hadn't been by. Now I wonder if it was the person who wrote the letter."

"You would know if the person was Valerie?"

"I hope I would. Though after fifteen years, who knows? Anyway, a scammer would claim to know Valerie or to be her 'representative'—a friend, or a lawyer."

"You do know how these things work, don't you?"

"Unfortunately, I do." He stood. "I wouldn't worry about that letter, though. If you ignore these people, they move on and look for an easier victim."

She tucked the letter back into the envelope and returned it to her purse. "Sorry to disturb your evening."

"No. That's okay. I didn't have any plans." He shoved his hands in the pockets of his jeans. "I was getting ready to make dinner. You want to stay and eat with me?"

"Oh, uh…"

"Sorry, you probably have plans."

"No. I'd be happy to stay. I can help too."

"Then come into the kitchen, and let's see what we've got to work with."

Together, they assembled a meal of pasta, chicken and vegetables. As they worked, they talked about everything but Valerie—his love of climbing, her passion for gardening, his experience with search and rescue, and her volunteer position working with high school journalism students.

"Are you seeing anyone?" she asked when the conversation lulled. Maybe the question was a bit forward, but she was dying to know. And she hadn't seen any sign of a romantic interest around his place.

He didn't look up from draining the pasta. "No. Are you?"

"No. I broke up with a guy a few months ago."

He dumped the pasta in a bowl and carried the bowl to the table. "Is that good? Bad?"

"A little sad." She sat in the chair across from him at the table. "We'd been together awhile. But it wasn't working out." They had fallen into a pattern of fighting more than they got along. "Breaking up was the right thing to do."

"But lonely when you're used to having someone around," he said.

Was that the voice of experience speaking or just someone who was very empathetic? "I've managed to avoid long-term relationships," he continued. "I'm not the easiest guy to get along with."

"You haven't thrown up any red flags for me." Her cheeks warmed. She hadn't meant that to sound like she was sizing him up for potential-mate material. "I mean, I haven't noticed any upsetting tendencies—a bad temper or substance abuse, or narcissism."

He laughed. "According to several exes, I don't trust people, I don't confide in people and I don't care enough about people."

"Harsh."

"Yeah, well, who's to say they haven't been right? Not everyone has to be part of a couple."

"You're absolutely right." She raised her wineglass. "To being happy with yourself."

"To being happy with yourself." He smiled, and his gaze met hers, and something lurched inside her, an internal shift that signaled she might be even happier with a certain untrusting, unconfiding but definitely not uncaring man.

Chapter Six

Elisabeth couldn't believe how great it felt to be in the mountains again. Was it possible she had been missing this without even realizing it? Amid all this bare rock and immense sky, anything seemed possible, as if the world truly had no limits. She continued up the trail, climbing higher and higher, thighs burning, lungs straining for breath. Obviously, she needed more time to acclimate to the altitude, but she was in pretty good shape, considering she hadn't spent much time on athletic pursuits.

She stopped and assessed her surroundings. There was a flat-sided dike jutting up from the adjacent rock like a jagged tooth. And there was a big boulder, lichen spattering the surface in green and white and orange. She climbed the rock, scrambling a little for purchase, and stood atop it. She stared at the clump of pinions below, in a kind of trance for a long moment.

She snapped out of it and turned to face the dike. She pulled out her phone and took a few pictures to document the scene; then she headed back down the trail. She met only a few people on the way down—a couple and a larger group of friends. No little kids. Did families not come backpacking up here anymore?

Back in town, she grabbed a decent veggie wrap from

the coffee shop at the Gold Nugget Hotel, then walked down the street to a real estate office she had spotted earlier. She stopped on the sidewalk outside Brown Realty to study the flyers tacked to the window, all for overpriced vacation homes, luxury condos and one huge ranch that was listed for over a billion dollars. Did people really pay those kinds of prices to live here? If that was the case, she might stick around a little longer and meet some of those wealthy people.

A chime announced her arrival as she pushed open the door. A man who was the sole occupant of the place looked up from behind the desk and smiled. "Hi," he said. "Can I help you?"

He was maybe a little older than her, his long dark hair pulled back in a ponytail. He wore a tailored white shirt, sleeves rolled up to reveal strong forearms, and dark jeans that definitely hadn't come from the nearest discount store. Paul would approve of this man's style. "I'm looking for a place to rent in town," she said. "Just for a couple of months. A house or condo. Something nice."

"We have several beautiful vacation properties available for short-term rentals." The man stood and extended his hand. "I'm Mitch."

"I'm Elisabeth." His fingers were cool against hers, his grip firm but not crushing. And he looked her in the eye with a direct gaze. A sizzle of attraction raced through her. No ring on his finger.

"Have a seat, Elisabeth, and I'll show you what we have available." He sat also, and swiveled the computer monitor so they both could see it. "Do you have a particular location in mind?"

"There's a condo complex by the river. Riverside. Do you have anything there?"

"We do have a few units available in that property," Mitch said. "Though they require a six-month lease."

"If they're vacant, maybe we can negotiate something shorter."

"I can't promise anything, but why don't we take a look?"

He bent over the keyboard, typing with two fingers, but rapidly. She studied him, feeling the sizzle of awareness again. Maybe there were advantages to sticking around town that she hadn't yet considered.

"Here are some interior shots of one of the units," he said. "It's a top floor, corner unit, so a little more privacy. As you can see, it has updated appliances and a modern, airy interior. You'd be close to the river and the hiking and biking trails, and just a few minutes from town. Another few minutes to the highway and access to both Junction, an hour to the north, and the miles of trails in the backcountry. Hiking and jeeping in the summer, rock and ice climbing, winter skiing. Fly-fishing, photography, camping—we offer everything in the way of outdoor adventure."

He spoke with a natural enthusiasm that helped negate the salesman's spiel. "I like the condo," she said. "Could we drive over there and take a look?"

"Of course. Do you want to see any others before we go?"

"No. That's the one I want."

"What about the six-month lease?" he asked.

"I'm sure we can work something out." She could always agree to the lease, then leave whenever she wanted without paying the rest of the rent. She knew how to disappear so that they would never find her to sue for the rest of the money.

"Let me forward the phones and lock up here, and I'll be set," he said.

She waited by the entrance while he took care of these tasks, then followed him out the door. After he had locked up, she moved closer and slipped her arm through his. "After we see the condo, maybe you can show me around town," she said. "Then I'd love to buy you a drink."

Extra heat sparked in his smile, and he covered her hand with his own and squeezed it. "That sounds like a great idea, Elisabeth."

"I'm full of great ideas." So many, and so few people to truly appreciate her greatness. But she had learned to never sell herself short. Other people had failed her, but that was no reason to ever fail herself.

SUMMER SATURDAYS WERE busy days on the backroads and trails around Eagle Mountain, which meant they were also busy for search and rescue volunteers. The first call that day came in just before 11:00 a.m. A young man had fallen from the rocks above Rocky Falls. "The family member who called in the accident says the young man—fifteen—is responsive but in pain," Danny told the volunteers who assembled at search and rescue headquarters. "He thinks the boy—his nephew—might have broken bones."

"How did he happen to fall, do we know?" volunteer Chris Mercer asked. An artist who wore blue streaks in her dark hair, Chris had several years' experience with SAR but wasn't an elite climber or a medical professional. She was simply dedicated and hardworking, willing to do the mundane driving, fetching, carrying and following orders that made up the bulk of a volunteer's efforts.

Danny grimaced. "He climbed up onto the rocks to pose for a picture and slipped."

"The rocks behind the sign that says 'Danger: Do Not Climb on Rocks'?" Harper Stevens asked.

"Yep." Danny raised his voice to address them all. "Let's hustle, everyone."

As they were loading their gear, Bethany slipped in next to Vince. "Hi." She flashed a smile, her eyes not meeting his. "This is the first call I've been on. I'm a little nervous."

"That's natural," Vince said. "Just do what you're told and pitch in whenever you can." He handed her a plastic bin full of climbing helmets. "Find a place to stow these in the Beast there." He pointed to the specially outfitted Jeep used for rescue operations. "I'm going to get more supplies."

"I think you have an admirer," Ryan said when Vince returned to the supply closet for another load. "I saw the new girl, Bethany, making eyes at you."

"'Making eyes'? Seriously, what does that even mean?" Vince slung a coil of rope over one shoulder.

"Bet she'd go out with you if you asked her," Ryan said. "Just saying."

He glanced back and saw Bethany standing where he had left her, still watching him. He quickly turned around. "Not interested," he said. Bethany was cute and probably really sweet, but there was no spark there. Not like when he looked at Tammy. "Come on," he said. "Let's get this stuff loaded so we can head out."

The young man who had fallen got off lucky, with a broken leg and some cracked ribs. The search and rescue team climbed the trail to the top of the falls and identified a point from which Hannah and Ryan Welch could be lowered on ropes to the teen, Lance. At first, he denied climbing on the rocks, though eventually he admitted to ignoring the signs and boosting himself up on the boulder for a selfie with the waterfall in the background. "Am I going to be, like, disabled or something?" he asked, his expression stricken.

"You should heal just fine," Hannah said as she fitted his leg with a splint. Once the leg was stabilized, she and

Ryan fitted him with neck and back braces and a helmet, then helped him into a litter and wrapped him up warmly.

Meanwhile, up on the trail, Vince worked with Eldon, Tony and Sheri to rig a rope-and-pulley system for getting their patient back onto the trail. Once they had lifted him safely out of the canyon, another group of volunteers took over to transport him to the waiting ambulance. The family—his mom, dad, uncle and sister—followed the litter team down.

As the remaining volunteers disassembled the rigging and packed up to return to headquarters, Vince paused to look over at the sign that cautioned people against climbing on the rocks. "I feel like someone should write in 'We really mean it' underneath there," he said.

"It wouldn't work," Eldon said. He stuffed a brake bar into a carrying bag. "Kids that age think they're invincible. I did."

Unlike many of his peers, Vince had never known that feeling of invulnerability. What happened to Valerie had made him too aware of all the ways things could go wrong.

The group returned to SAR headquarters and were unloading gear when a second call came in. "Hikers with a medical emergency," Danny relayed after speaking with the emergency dispatcher. "Mount Wilson trail. A man with chest pains and a woman who's collapsed."

The words were like a shot of adrenaline through the group. They hurried to reload the search and rescue Jeep, as well as several personal vehicles, with equipment and personnel for an urgent ride to the Mount Wilson trailhead. "They're within a mile of the top," Danny directed as they unloaded the vehicles and distributed gear for the trek up the slope. "A thirty-eight-year-old woman and a forty-six-year-old man. No history of heart trouble, but he's reporting chest pain and dizziness and disorientation."

"What about the woman?" Hannah asked.

"The report on her is that she's unable to continue hiking."

"I don't like the sound of either of those," Hannah said.

A solemn team started up the mountain. Tony and Sheri elected to jog ahead with an AED and first aid supplies. Caleb Garrison was next with a canister of oxygen, while the others followed as quickly as they could, spread out along the steep trail to one of the most popular peaks in the region. Other hikers on their way down squeezed over to the side to let them pass when they recognized the blue windbreakers with *Search and Rescue* emblazoned on the front and back. "Good luck!" some called after them.

It took two hours of hard hiking to reach the couple, who were stretched out to one side of the trail, a few concerned onlookers gathered around. Sheri, Tony, Caleb and Hannah were arranged around them, the man receiving oxygen while Sheri spoke with the woman. Vince slipped off his pack, which contained another canister of oxygen and various first aid supplies, and fished out his water bottle.

"What's the story?" he asked Harper, who had arrived ahead of him.

"Hannah doesn't think he's having a heart attack, but he'll need to be checked out at the hospital to be sure," Harper said. "Mostly I think they weren't well prepared for a hike like this and they overdid it. They don't have hats or sunscreen or enough water. They're sunburned and dehydrated and dealing with the altitude and exhaustion."

The couple did look miserable. They were sipping water and listening as Sheri and Danny addressed them each in turn. They were probably hearing about how most of their problems could have been prevented with simple precautions like sunscreen, water and an easier pace. But that didn't help them now. For that, they would get a free ride down the mountain in litters carried by Vince and his fellow volunteers, and a checkup at the hospital to ensure they truly were all right.

The trip down the trail was equally as solemn as the hike up, but without the urgency. Even a small adult was a heavy, awkward burden to carry. After consultation, Danny declared that the woman would walk down—with Bethany and Harper on either side to steady her, if need be—and her husband would be transported on the litter. His chest pains had subsided, but no one wanted to chance their return. The litter was fitted with a large wheel to support part of the weight and help it roll along the ground, but it still required a volunteer at each corner to help steady and balance it. The position was awkward and uncomfortable, and volunteers switched off every half mile.

Meanwhile, the woman moaned and complained the whole way down. Vince decided that as much as maneuvering the litter made his back and knees ache, he preferred that duty.

The sun was sinking behind the mountains by the time they made it to the trailhead. The couple headed off in an ambulance, and the volunteers reloaded their gear. Some of the group announced they were going out for beer and pizza. "Are you going out?" Bethany asked as Vince was shouldering his pack to head to his car.

"Not tonight," he said. All he wanted was a hot shower and to stretch out on the sofa, where he would likely fall asleep. "But you should go, if you want. It'll be a great way to get to know people."

She looked over toward the group—Ryan and Eldon, Caleb, and a few others. "I don't know."

"Suit yourself." He shrugged on the pack and headed out. He drove to his condo, parked, and collected his mail before he walked to his door and unlocked it. Inside, he shed

his shoes, pack and SAR windbreaker, then stood sorting
through the mail. Mostly junk, but a colorful postcard caught
his eye. A larger-than-life cartoon Viking stood beside an im-
possibly buxom and equally cartoonish female Viking. *Welcome to Williams's Valhalla-Land!* proclaimed large green
letters above them.

Vince stared, heart pounding. He and Valerie and their
parents had stopped at this roadside attraction, somewhere
in Minnesota or Michigan, on a road trip to visit his dad's
brother and his family on the Upper Peninsula the summer before Valerie disappeared. Somewhere, pasted into an
album tucked into his parents' bookshelf, was a photograph
his mother had snapped of him and Valerie, posing with these
same cartoon Vikings.

He flipped the card over and read the message, in loopy
cursive handwriting: *Hello, Vince the Viking. I bet you're
surprised to hear from me. V.*

Chapter Seven

"Slow down, Mitch. I can hardly understand you, you're talking so fast." Tammy juggled her phone and the salad she had been carrying to her kitchen table when her brother called Saturday evening.

"I met this great girl—*woman*. Her name is Elisabeth. She came into my office looking for a rental, and we hit it off. We had drinks afterwards, and we're going to have dinner tomorrow night."

Tammy sat at the table. Her brother wasn't normally this effusive. In fact, he rarely talked about the women he dated. "Wow, she must be special," she said.

"I think so." She could hear the smile in his voice. "I hope you'll meet her soon."

"You said she was looking for a rental. Is she new in town?"

"She's here for several months, but I'm hoping to talk her into staying longer."

"Where is she from?"

"Somewhere in the Midwest, I think. We didn't talk about that."

"What *did* you talk about?"

He laughed. "She asked a lot about me, and about Eagle Mountain. But she told me a few things about herself. She said her father just died and left her some money, so she's taking the opportunity to see more of the country. And she likes to hike—we talked about checking out a few of the local trails while she's here."

"It sounds like the two of you really clicked."

"We did. I've never met anyone who is so easy to talk to. I tried to talk her into having dinner with me tonight too, but she said she had things she needed to do. I thought at first maybe I had come on too strong, but then she said she'd love to go out with me tomorrow night, so that was a relief."

"I'll look forward to meeting her." She took a bite of salad and chewed, angling away from the phone as Mitch told her more about the wonderful Elisabeth.

Her phone beeped, and she checked the screen. "I have to go, Mitch," she said. "I have another call coming in, and I need to take it."

"A breaking news story for the paper?" he asked.

"Someone connected with an article that I need to talk to." Not a complete lie.

"All right, then. I'll talk to you later."

"Have fun tomorrow night." She ended the call and answered the incoming one. "Hey, Vince," she said.

"Do you still have that note that was supposedly from Valerie?" he asked.

"I think so. Why?"

"Because I got a postcard today." His voice broke, and the silence that followed made her think he was struggling to pull himself together.

"Vince, are you all right?" she asked.

"The postcard—it had something on it only Valerie, or someone who knew us, would know about," he said.

She sat up straighter. "Do you think Valerie sent my note and your postcard?"

"I don't know what to think. I mean, if she is alive, why not just pick up the phone and call? Or come to see me in person?"

"Have your parents heard anything? It seems like she would want to contact them too."

"If they have, they haven't told me about it. And I'm too afraid to call and upset them. What if this is just another scam?"

"Maybe you should contact the sheriff's office," she said.

"Maybe. Before I do that, could you come over, and bring the note you received? Or I could come there. I thought we could compare the signature and decide if it's the same person."

"The note is at the newspaper office," she said. "Why don't you meet me there?"

"Great. I'll see you in a few minutes."

She ended the call, then sat for a moment, her salad untouched. The reporter side of her was intrigued by the turn this story was taking. But she hadn't missed the pain in Vince's voice. She wanted to protect her friend while still getting to the bottom of what could be major news.

VINCE WAITED ON the sidewalk outside the newspaper office. A few people passed on their way to the pizza place at the end of the block, but otherwise this part of town was quiet. The sun had set, but it wasn't yet full dark. The silhouettes of the mountains above town stood out against the gray sky. The tops of those peaks were miles away, yet they looked almost close enough to touch.

He slipped off his backpack and felt in the side pocket, where he had tucked the postcard. His sister couldn't have sent it, could she? Why now, after so many years? And why be so vague?

A blue Subaru zipped around the corner and pulled to the curb in front of Vince. Tammy got out. She looked harried, her cheeks flushed, her blouse half-untucked and her hair a little mussed. "I hope you haven't been waiting long," she said.

"Not long." He waited behind her while she unlocked the door, then tapped a code into the alarm keypad beside it.

"Come on back here to my desk." She moved through the office, flipping light switches as she went, until she reached a large desk crowded with a desktop computer and stacks of notebooks and loose sheets of paper. "The letter is in the file here," she said, and pulled open a bottom desk drawer. She rummaged among the contents of the drawer, then stood, waving a piece of paper. "I never throw anything away," she said. "As you can tell by the state of my desk."

She sank into the desk chair, and Vince sat in a straight-backed wooden chair across from her. She set the letter on the desk between them and smoothed out the folds. "Could I see the postcard you received?" she asked.

He opened the backpack and handed the card to her. She smiled as she studied the cartoon on the front, then turned it over to read the message on the back. "'Vince the Viking'?" she asked.

He grimaced. "The summer before Valerie disappeared—when we were both nine—we took a family trip to the Upper Peninsula to visit my dad's brother, Ricky. On the way, we stopped at every tourist attraction my dad could find—windmills and arrowhead collections and little museums." He nodded to the postcard. "And Valhalla-Land."

Tammy's smile vanished and her eyebrows drew together. "It would be a wild coincidence for someone who didn't know about that trip to send this to you out of the blue."

"I think so," he said. "And it's not just Valhalla-Land.

After the trip, Valerie and I called each other 'Vince the Viking' and 'Valerie the Viking' for weeks afterwards. No one else would know that. I mean, my mom and dad would, if they even remember. And maybe Uncle Ricky. But they wouldn't pretend to be Valerie."

Tammy turned the postcard over. "This is postmarked in Junction, but it could have been mailed here in town. All our mail is routed through the Junction office. But that's a long way from Valhalla-Land."

"Whoever sent it must have brought it with them," he said.

"Could you order something like this online?" Tammy asked.

"Even if you could, you would have to know its significance to me and Valerie." He sat back, legs stretched out in front of him. "I'd forgotten all about that little pit stop on a long-ago vacation until I saw that card."

She laid the card beside the letter on the desk and leaned over to study it more closely. "It's signed the same way as my note—just the single V," she said.

"I thought so too. But if it's Valerie, why not sign her whole name?"

"Do you think your parents still have a sample of her handwriting?"

"Probably. But she was ten. A person's handwriting changes as they get older, doesn't it?"

"I don't know." She sat back. "Do you think you should contact your parents? I'm sure if we go to the sheriff's department with these notes, they'll want to talk to your parents as well."

Vince blew out a breath. "I don't want to upset them, but better me than a call from a sheriff's deputy." He took out his phone.

His mother answered on the second ring. "Hello, Vince," she said, cheerful. Glad to hear from him.

"Hi, Mom. I'm not interrupting anything, am I?"

"No, I'm just sitting here trying to read this book that isn't all that interesting. It's for my book club, and it's supposed to be a big bestseller, but I must not be the intended audience."

"Is Dad there?"

"No, he had a meeting. Do you want me to ask him to call you tomorrow, or can I help you with something?"

He took a deep breath. He saw no way to ease into the subject. "Have you gotten any letters from someone claiming to be Valerie?" he asked.

"You mean recently?"

"Yes."

"No, dear. Years ago we received a couple of letters that were vague and rambling. We showed them to someone from the Center for Missing and Exploited Children. They told us they were almost certainly a scam. Other parents had received similar letters."

"I didn't know," he said.

"You were still young. We didn't see any reason to involve you. Why are you asking about this now?"

He glanced across the desk at Tammy. She was watching him intently. "I got a postcard from someone who sounded like they could be Valerie," he said. "It was just signed with the letter V."

"Oh my. I'm sure it's because of the article in the paper. It was a good article, of course, but this kind of attention seems to bring out the worst in people. What did the postcard say?"

He picked up the card. "Do you remember that summer we went to Uncle Ricky's place?"

"The summer you were nine. That was a fun trip."

"We stopped at a place called Valhalla-Land. With a bunch of Viking stuff."

"Oh my, yes. So kitschy. But you kids loved it."

"Valerie and I called each other Vikings for weeks after that."

His mom laughed. "I'd forgotten about that, but you did. Vince the Viking and Valerie the Viking. But what made you remember that?"

"This postcard has a picture of Valhalla-Land. And on the back, it says 'Hello to Vince the Viking.'"

His mother drew in her breath sharply but said nothing.

"Mom! Are you okay?"

"I'm… I'm fine. Just a little surprised. It's such an odd thing to write. And how would anyone know about that?"

"I don't know. The reporter who wrote the story for the paper, Tammy Patterson, received a note too. Hers was more generic. All about how she got things wrong in her story and 'You were sold a bunch of lies.' She and I think we should show these to the sheriff, just in case someone is trying to scam us. But I wanted to talk to you first."

"Yes, you should show them to the sheriff," she said. "Not that it will do any good. No one ever caught any of the other people who tried to swindle us. There are some evil people in this world who will take advantage of a family's grief."

"Tomorrow we'll talk to Sheriff Walker or one of his deputies," Vince said. "I'll let you know what they say."

"I'll tell your father when he gets in. It's odd. And upsetting. What if this really is Valerie, reaching out to us after all these years?"

"Why send teasing notes?" he asked. "Why not just show up and say, 'Here I am'?"

"I don't know. Maybe it's a kind of game. Valerie did always like games and teasing. The day she disappeared, we thought she was hiding from us, playing a joke."

"If she's alive, she's twenty-five," Vince said. "Too old for silly games."

"I don't know what to think," his mom said.

"I'll let you know what the sheriff says."

They said good-night, and he ended the call. He felt worse than ever.

"Do you want me to go with you to the sheriff's department tomorrow?" Tammy asked.

"They'll want to talk to you too." He looked around the room, at the silent computers and framed front pages of past issues of the *Eagle Mountain Examiner*. "Are you going to write about this for the paper?"

He couldn't read her expression. Was that hurt in her eyes? "Not unless something comes of it that's newsworthy," she said.

"What would that be?"

"I don't know. If they catch someone trying to scam you."

"Or if Valerie actually is alive and well."

"People do show up sometimes," Tammy said. "There was a case last year where a woman had been living in Europe with her kidnapper for years. I'm not trying to get your hopes up," she hastened to add. "I'm just saying that's one possibility."

"Yeah. I guess we'll find out." He stood. "Thanks for meeting with me. I'll let you know in the morning when I can go with you to the sheriff. I need to check my work schedule."

He left the building. She followed, locking up behind them. "Do you want to go for a drink?" she asked. "Or coffee?"

"No. I need to go home."

"All right. I'll see you tomorrow." She hesitated, then patted his arm. "I'm sorry my article pulled this person—whoever they are—out of the woodwork. Especially if it's someone who wants to hurt you."

"It's not your fault. And maybe it *is* Valerie." He didn't believe that, but it was something positive to cling to, at least for a little while. Over the years, he had thought about what it might be like to see his sister again, but after so long it was hard to picture her as anything but the rambunctious ten-year-old she had been. A grown Valerie would be a stranger to him. She would still be his sister—his twin. But they would have lost so much of their shared history. Would she even be someone he liked? Worse—would she like him, or what he had become in her absence?

Ten years ago

"I LEFT DINNER for you in the refrigerator. Leave the plate covered and heat it in the microwave for three minutes." Mom fussed about the kitchen, wiping down the counter and putting stray glasses and silverware in the dishwasher as she talked. "If you need anything, call the Wilsons next door for help. Don't open the door to strangers. And don't stay up too late watching TV. You know you have school tomorrow."

"Mom, I know how to look after myself. I'm not some little kid," Vince protested. At fifteen, he towered over his five-foot, two-inch mom, and was the same height as his dad. Any day now, he'd probably start shaving.

"I know, dear." His mom stilled, looking as if she wasn't happy about this news. "I just want you to be careful. I couldn't cope if anything happened to you."

Inwardly, Vince cringed, though he tried not to show how much he resented statements like this. He got it—his parents had lost one child and were terrified of losing another. They were hyperprotective of him, so much so that even leaving him alone for a few hours while they enjoyed a rare evening out with friends was a big deal. But none of his friends had as many rules and curfews as he did. It wasn't fair. But the one time he had tried to point this out, his mother had gotten all teary and said it wasn't fair that Valerie disappeared and they never knew what happened to her. After that, he gave up trying to reason with his parents and settled for breaking their rules whenever he could. Tonight, for instance, his friend Jackson Greenway was coming over. Their plan was to smoke a joint and watch a porn video Jackson had stolen from his older brother Parker, who was nineteen and had his own condo. They were going to order pizza and maybe call these sisters Jackson had met. His parents would be horrified if they knew any of this, which was kind of the point.

He hugged his mom. "Don't worry," he said. "I'll be safe here. You and Dad have a good time."

She gave him a wobbly smile and patted his back. "You're a fine son," she said. "Your father and I are so proud of you. You know that, don't you?"

He had done a lot to make his parents proud. He made good grades and was a top player on a regional youth lacrosse team. When he did break the rules, he made sure not to get caught, and he had never gotten into serious trouble. It didn't make up for Valerie being gone, but it was something.

He waved from the front door as they pulled out of the driveway, then slipped out his phone and called Jackson to tell him the coast was clear.

Twenty minutes later, Jackson's mother's Camry eased down the street, the throbbing bass from the stereo rattling the windows. Six months older than Vince, Jackson had his driver's license, and his parents let him borrow his mother's car whenever he wanted, as long as he topped off the gas tank.

Jackson—taller even than Vince, with long, thin arms and legs and blond hair past his shoulders—parked at the curb, then exited the car with the pizza box in one hand and a DVD and a bag of weed in the other. "Are we ready to party?" he asked.

"Ready." Vince held the door open wide. "We have the place to ourselves for at least four hours."

"Sweet!" Jackson breezed in and set the pizza on the bar that separated the kitchen from the living room. "And look what I got to go with our pizza." He fished in the pockets of his baggy cargo shorts and pulled out two cans of beer. "I snagged them from the garage refrigerator on my way out. My dad will never miss them."

"Let me grab some plates for the pizza," Vince said. "I'm starving."

They had popped the tops on the beer and were digging into their first slices of pizza when the Shepherd's house phone rang.

"Don't answer it," Jackson said. "It's probably just some phone solicitor or a politician asking for your vote."

"I have to answer it," Vince said. "It might be my mom, with some last-minute instruction about dinner or something." He moved to the phone on the kitchen wall and picked up the receiver. "Hello?"

"Hello? Vince, is that you?"

A cold shiver raced up his spine. "Hello?" he said. "Who is this?" His mind played tricks on him sometimes. He would be in a crowded hallway at school and would think he'd heard Valerie's voice, only to turn around and discover it was someone else. Once, after a lacrosse game, he had followed a teenage girl all the way to the parking lot because something about how she looked from the back was so familiar. Then she had turned around and spotted him, and he had to pretend he was merely retrieving something from his car.

"It's Valerie. Don't you remember me?" The person on the

other end of the line began to sob. "I need you to help me, Vince."

"Where are you?" he asked. Then: "Who are you, really?"

The line went dead. Vince stared at the receiver in his hand.

"Dude, your face went all white," Jackson said. "You're not going to faint, are you?"

"How do you call back the last number you talked to?" he asked.

"Star-six-nine." Jackson's chair scraped loudly against the floor as he shoved it back and stood. "What's going on? Who was that on the phone?"

"I don't know." He punched in *69 and waited while the phone rang. And rang. And rang. After ten rings, he hung up.

Jackson was standing beside him now. "You don't look so hot," he said. "Who was that calling?"

"She said she was Valerie."

Jackson's eyes widened. "Your dead sister?"

"We don't know for sure she's dead, but yeah. She knew my name, and she said she was Valerie."

"Did it sound like her? What you remember?"

"It did." But was that because it was her, or because he wanted it to be her? "I think you'd better go," he said. "I need to call my parents."

He thought Jackson would argue, but instead, he patted Vince's back. "I can stay here if you want. You can tell your folks you called me for moral support. We'll hide the beer and stuff before they get home."

"Thanks, but I'll be okay by myself."

Jackson gathered up the beer and pizza, the pot and the DVD, and said goodbye. When he was gone, Vince braced himself and called his dad's cell phone. "I had a call just now," he said. "From someone claiming to be Valerie. She

said she needed help, and she started crying. It sounded real."
A sob broke free on the last word. He couldn't help it.

"We'll be right there," his dad said.

His parents came home right away. Vince had pulled himself together by the time they arrived, but he could tell his mom had been crying. Her eyes were red and puffy, and when she hugged him, she held on too tightly, for a little too long.

He told them about the call, and they contacted the local police and the FBI agent who had worked with them when Valerie first went missing. The cops arrived, then two FBI agents. They matched the number from the call to a pay phone in Nebraska, then said the pay phone had been vandalized, probably before that call was made, though they couldn't be sure.

They never heard from the caller again, and everyone agreed it had likely been a scam. But for months afterward, Vince replayed the call in his head. Valerie's voice, begging him to help her.

Chapter Eight

"We can take this into evidence, but without more context, there's not a lot we can do." Sheriff Walker faced Tammy and Vince across his neat desk Sunday morning, the letter and postcard side by side on the almost-empty expanse of oak. "Unfortunately, it's not unusual for twisted people to prey on the families of crime victims this way."

"We don't know that Valerie's disappearance was a crime." Vince flushed when Travis turned to look at him.

"That's true," Travis said. "But it's a crime to pretend to be someone else for the purpose of extorting money or other compensation."

"The letter writer hasn't asked for anything," Tammy said.

"Not yet." Travis considered the letters once more. "If you receive any other correspondence like this, handle it as little as possible. We might be able to recover prints or DNA."

They promised to keep the sheriff informed of any developments and left his office. Outside, on the sidewalk, Vince pulled out his keys. "I have to go," he said. "I promised my parents I'd have lunch with them."

"Before you go, there's something I need to say." Tammy had been rehearsing this little speech all morning, and she needed to get it out before she lost nerve.

He stopped and turned to face her, expression wary.

"You asked me last night if I'm going to write about this," she said.

"Have you changed your mind?"

"No." She shook her head. "Not unless you want me to. If you think it will help us find who did this, I will."

"No. The last thing I want right now is more publicity. It draws out the scammers."

"I'm your friend, Vince," she said. "First. Reporter, second. I want to make sure you understand that. I want you to feel free to talk to me without fear of what you say ending up in the paper." Having him believe anything other than that hurt more than she wanted to admit.

"Thanks," he said. "I appreciate it."

"Good. I wanted to make sure you knew that."

Embarrassed now, she turned and led the way down the sidewalk toward the lot where they had parked their vehicles. They hadn't gone far before she spotted a familiar figure. "Hey, Mitch." She waved.

Her brother stopped and waited for her to catch up. She turned back to Vince. "Vince, this is my brother, Mitch. Mitch, this is Vince Shepherd."

The two men shook hands. "How's it going?" Vince asked.

"I'm headed over to Riverside Condos." Mitch glanced at Tammy. "Elisabeth signed a lease on an empty unit there, and I want to make sure there's no problem with the paperwork."

"Vince lives at Riverside," Tammy said.

Mitch grinned. "Then you'll see me around. At least, I hope you will."

"Mitch is so gone on his new client," Tammy said.

"Elisabeth is a special person," Mitch said. He checked his watch. "Gotta run. Nice to meet you, Vince."

Mitch loped away. They were at their cars now; Tammy

turned to Vince. "Let me know if anything else happens," she said. "Because I'm your friend. Not because I'm a reporter."

He took a step back, hands in his pockets. "Thanks. Um, maybe we could have dinner later."

She fought back a grin. "I'd like that."

"Just…as friends," he added.

"Sure." It wasn't all she wanted, but it would do. For now.

As A ROOKIE with just a few months of search and rescue experience under his belt, Vince saw every call as a new challenge. Though veterans might approach another auto accident or fallen hiker as the type of incident they had competently dealt with dozens of times before, Vince's mind raced with a review of everything he had learned about the protocol for this type of emergency, and the awareness that one misstep could potentially jeopardize someone's life.

No one was looking at their mission Tuesday evening as routine, however. Rescuers lined the road above Carson Canyon and followed the beam of a handheld spotlight until it came to rest on a pickup truck snagged in an almost-vertical position on the sharply sloping canyon wall. The truck's front end was smashed, the windshield shattered, the back bumper and half the rear-cargo area extending out into the darkness beyond—a canyon that was easily a hundred yards deep. "It looks like the front axle is snagged over that boulder." Danny lowered the binoculars he had been using to survey the scene and handed them to Tony. "See what you think."

"I don't see anything to secure chains to," Ryan said. "How are we going to stabilize the wreck enough to make it safe for us to go down there?"

"Shine that light into the cab," Tony said.

Grace, who was holding the light, shifted the beam to illuminate the cab.

"Looks like at least two people in the vehicle," Tony said. "Still secured by seat belts. They're not moving, so they're either dead or unconscious."

"We need to get a wrecker out here," Caleb said. "They could hook onto the frame with chains and it wouldn't go anywhere."

"One of us will have to climb down and hook it up," Eldon said. "We've done it before."

"We've done it before," Ryan said, "but not to a vehicle in that kind of precarious position."

"And not in the dark."

"Let's get some lights out here," Danny said. He took out his phone. "I'm going to call for a wrecker. But I want you to start rigging for the rescue. Approach it as if we don't have a wrecker available. You need to secure the vehicle, get the rescuers down safely, and lift out the driver and passenger."

"See if a helicopter is available," Sheri said. "It might be easier to lift the victims out by air than to try to drag them up this steep slope."

Danny acknowledged this and spoke into his phone. Ryan turned to Vince. "Come help us with the rigging."

"Could I help?" Bethany spoke up.

"Have you done any climbing training yet?" Ryan asked. "Not yet."

"Then it's probably better that you help with setting up the portable work lights. Everything will make more sense to you after you've got a little more training under your belt."

"Oh, uh, sure." She gave a wobbly smile and hurried away.

Ryan smirked. "Don't say anything," Vince warned. He wasn't in the mood for teasing—no matter how good natured—over the new girl's infatuation with him.

Ryan held up his hands. "I didn't say a thing."

Ryan, Vince and several others set to work constructing

the intricate series of ropes, chains, anchors, pulleys, knots, brake bars, carabiners and other hardware to construct a spiderweb of lines that would enable volunteers to travel safely up and down the steep slope.

Two trucks from the highway department pulled up with a bank of work lights that did a better job of illuminating the accident scene. Close on their heels, Bud O'Brien arrived with his largest wrecker, which featured a long boom that could extend over the canyon. A portly man in his late fifties with a wad of chewing tobacco puffing out one cheek, Bud peered over the edge at the smashed truck. "I can get it out of there," he said. "But one of you will have to hook it up."

Danny delegated Ryan and Eldon to make the initial climb down. Once the vehicle was secure, Tony and Sheri would follow, with Caleb and Vince on standby if they needed more assistance. "We'll need to package the victims for transport on the helicopter flying in from Delta. The chopper will set them down in the road, and we'll transfer to an ambulance."

"Any response from the truck?" Vince asked.

"Nothing," Danny said. "I tried hailing them and got no reply. I thought I saw movement earlier, but it's difficult from this distance to be sure." He looked past Vince. "I think Bud has the wrecker in place now." He raised his voice. "All right, everybody. Let's do this!"

Vince positioned himself across from Caleb to monitor the rigging as first Ryan, then Eldon descended. He found himself holding his breath as Ryan neared the vehicle. One false move might send the truck plummeting the rest of the way into the canyon. From here, he couldn't see the people inside. Maybe it was a good thing they were unconscious, since that made it less likely they would move about and possibly dislodge the vehicle.

With Ryan in place just above and behind the truck, Eldon

started his descent. Vince watched carefully, trying to absorb everything. Maybe one day he would be the one setting the rigging or even making the descent. He had a little experience climbing, though nowhere near the training Sherri, Ryan and some of the others had completed in high-angle rescue.

When Eldon had almost reached Ryan, Danny signaled to Bud, who began lowering the heavy cable and hook from the boom, which was extended out over the canyon. Eldon snagged the hook, then prepared to crawl beneath the truck.

Bud radioed down. "Be sure to attach that to the frame, not the axle."

"Understood," Eldon said. "That truck better not slip and take me with it."

"We've got you," Caleb called over the radio. Eldon and Ryan were both attached to safety lines tethered to anchors at the top of the cliff.

A cheer rose up when Eldon emerged from beneath the truck, thumbs up. Then he and Ryan approached the truck's cab, one on either side. They had to hold on to the vehicle in order to balance on the narrow ledge. Ryan cleared away broken glass and leaned into the driver's side of the vehicle. A moment later he leaned out again. "A driver and one passenger. The driver is unconscious, lacerations on his head and face. The passenger is female. No pulse. We're going to need the Jaws down here to get them out."

The mood among the volunteers sobered at the news that the passenger was dead, but they set to work securing the hydraulic extractor, more commonly known as the Jaws of Life, for cutting into the truck to make it easier to free the driver and passenger. They attached the tool to a line, and Tony and Sheri took it down when they descended.

"This is the scariest thing I've seen," Bethany said as she

and Vince watched their fellow volunteers work on cutting the truck cab apart. "One slip and the whole truck might go over, and everyone down there with it."

"Part of me is glad I'm not down there," Vince said. "But it's hard to be up here too, wishing I could do more to help."

"Somebody has to be up here, making sure nothing goes wrong with the rigging," she said.

"You're right." He glanced below again as Tony and Eldon eased the driver from the truck cab onto a backboard. "I'll be glad when everyone is up top safely."

"I hear you."

Someone called to Bethany, and she moved away. Vince relaxed a little. Bethany was nice, but her obvious interest in him made him uncomfortable. She hadn't said or done anything out of line, but every time he turned around, she was either standing next to him or watching from across the room. Others besides Ryan had noticed. He didn't want to be rude to her, but he wished she would back off a little.

He focused again on the scene below. The volunteers fitted the driver with a helmet, neck brace and an oxygen mask and strapped him into a litter. They had a radio conversation with Danny, who, in addition to being the search and rescue captain, was also a registered nurse.

A heavy throb signaled the arrival of the rescue helicopter. The beam from its searchlight had them shielding their eyes from the glare. The chopper swept in, then hovered over the crash site and lowered a cable. The team below had affixed lines to the litter and attached these to the cable from the helicopter. At a signal from Tony, the helicopter rose and ferried the injured man to the middle of the closed road, where another team of volunteers helped lower the litter to the ground, unfastened it from the cable and carried it to a waiting ambulance.

The helicopter headed for the canyon again, this time to retrieve the black bag containing the body of the passenger. This second transfer accomplished, the volunteers collected their gear and ascended, one at a time, up the canyon walls. Vince, Caleb and Chris monitored the climbers. As soon as everyone was up top and out of their climbing harnesses, they began the tedious chore of disassembling all the rigging and putting everything neatly away, ready to be used in the next emergency.

"How did the passenger die?" Caleb asked Tony as they disconnected various pieces of hardware from the climbing ropes they had used to assemble the rigging.

"Can't say for sure," Tony said. "But maybe a broken neck. The driver had a head injury. I think he may have banged his head into the window. Everything in the vehicle was thrown around. I think it was a pretty violent descent."

Vince shuddered, imagining. This was the first call where the real threat of danger had superseded the adrenaline rush of helping someone out under challenging conditions. Today, there had been a real threat of harm to everyone involved. His worries over a couple of annoying notes seem petty in contrast.

THE PASS WAS closed by the time Tammy arrived. She had to park half a mile from the accident scene and hike up the road in the dark, past the line of cars waiting to get over the pass when it reopened, then past parked vehicles belonging to search and rescue volunteers, highway department employees and local law enforcement.

The accident site was lit up like a movie set, halogen lights on tall stands ringing a section of roadside and shining down into the canyon. Tammy stopped to take a picture, struck by the contrast of the bright lights and the shadowy cliffs. She was tucking her camera away when someone brushed past her. A slim, dark figure was running down the mountain, away from the accident. Tammy stared after the woman—she was sure it was a woman, though she had seen the figure for only a few seconds. Nothing about her was familiar, though.

She moved closer. Deputy Shane Ellis, who was standing beside his patrol vehicle, watching the search and rescue team work, waved in greeting. Tammy took out her camera once more and moved closer, in time to get a shot of volunteer Ryan Welch begin his descent into the canyon. She took a few more photographs of other volunteers. She didn't see Vince, but he would be easy to miss in the crowd with so many people milling around in the darkness.

She joined Shane by the sheriff's department SUV. Shane—a former professional baseball player who had surprised everyone by becoming a sheriff's deputy—nodded at her. "Good to see the local press reporting the latest news," he said.

She took out a notebook and pen. "What happened here?" she asked.

"It looks like a pickup truck came around that curve with too much speed." He pointed ahead of them, to a sharp curve on the highway. "He slid on loose gravel and went over the edge. The canyon walls are really steep in this section, and he must have had quite a ride. But he got lucky. The undercarriage of the vehicle hung up on a boulder."

"The driver was a male."

"We don't know for sure. And there appears to be at least one passenger. But until search and rescue takes a look, I don't have any more information."

She scribbled notes she hoped she would be able to read when she sat down tomorrow to write the story. "I saw Ryan Welch descending into the canyon," she said.

"He and Eldon Ramsey are going down to stabilize the

vehicle so rescuers can free the people inside the truck and assess their injuries," Shane said. "Bud O'Brien has his biggest wrecker out for the job."

The boom wrecker, lit up by the spotlights, would make an excellent shot for the paper. And Bud might like to have one to hang in his office. She started to move closer to take more photographs when Shane's next words stopped her. "I heard you got a note that was supposedly from Vince Shepherd's long-lost sister."

"I turned it into the sheriff," she said. "Do you know if he's learned anything more about whoever wrote it?"

"I don't think so," Shane said.

"Then I don't know any more than you do." She pushed away from the side of the SUV. "I'm going to get more photographs and talk to some of the rescuers."

She fired off a dozen more pictures, then climbed onto a boulder, which gave her a birds-eye view into the canyon. A couple of scraggly trees partially blocked her view of the wrecked truck, but she could see enough to feel a little queasy at the prospect of anyone trying to work around the smashed-up vehicle.

The loud chop of helicopter rotors drowned out the rumble of the wrecker's engine and the conversation of the volunteers. The rescue helicopter swept in and hovered on the edge of the canyon, the backwash from the rotors flinging loose gravel at onlookers and whipping back their hair. People tried to shield their eyes, but none of them looked away as a cable slowly lowered from the belly of the chopper. A few tense minutes later, the cable rose again, a litter bearing the figure of a person, wrapped like a mummy. A cheer rose from the crowd when the litter was safely inside.

Moments later, the cable lowered again. This time the trip was faster, as was the return journey. Another litter rose, but this one carried no securely wrapped figure—only a black plastic bag. The body bag meant one of the occupants of the truck hadn't made it.

Tammy moved in to speak with SAR Captain Danny Irwin. "Was there just the one fatality?" she asked.

"Yes. The passenger," Danny said "But the driver—a man—has a good chance of making it."

"Do we know who they are?" she asked.

Danny met her gaze. "We checked for ID, but I can't reveal that until their families are notified."

"Just tell me if they're locals," she said.

"They are not," he said.

Some of the tension that had been building since she had gotten the call about the accident lessened. The fatality was a tragedy, but not as wrenching as if it had been someone she knew. "What can you tell me about the rescue efforts?" she asked.

Danny straightened. "This was a highly technical rescue that put our training to the test," he said. "The truck was in a dangerous position, and our volunteers risked their lives to stabilize the vehicle and free the driver and passenger from the wreckage. This rescue involved everyone on-site, from those doing the climbing and rendering medical aid, to the volunteers who monitored the rigging, to those who provided backup support. This was an example of the teamwork Eagle Mountain Search and Rescue is known for."

"I got some great photos," Tammy said. "Everyone who lives here already knows how lucky we are to have such a great search and rescue group, but this kind of thing reminds them how awesome you all are."

"We're not doing it for the glory," Danny said. "But all that training and equipment isn't free. Anything that might net a few more donations is welcome."

Laughter from a group just beyond them distracted her. She looked past him. Was that Vince?

"Looking for someone?" Danny asked.

"Vince Shepherd. Is he here tonight?"

Danny looked around. "Vince is here somewhere."

"I'm sure I'll find him." She hurried away before Danny could ask why she wanted to speak with Vince. Even she wasn't completely sure of the answer to that question, except that she liked Vince a lot. She wanted to know him better. And she wanted him to like her.

She hadn't seen him since they had parted company after their interview with the sheriff Sunday morning. He hadn't followed up on his dinner invitation. She had picked up the phone to text him half a dozen times but had stopped herself from following through on the impulse. She wasn't going to chase a man who wasn't interested in her. Whatever happened between them would have to happen in its own time. If it didn't, well, maybe it wasn't meant to happen at all. Was that the coward in her, making excuses? Maybe so, but she was reluctant to let go of the notion that a real love should be strong enough to overcome the obstacles life put in its way. If it wasn't, what was the point? Life was so fragile and fleeting, why risk grabbing hold of something that was even more unreliable?

Vince shoved the last duffel of supplies into the back of the search and rescue vehicle known as the Beast. Six volunteers had snagged a ride to the scene in the specially outfitted Jeep, but he wasn't one of them. Instead, he and the rest of the crew had driven their personal vehicles. He had left his truck parked down the road from the accident site.

"I'm parked right behind you." Grace Wilcox fell into step beside him. Grace had been with the team a few months longer than he had, but he didn't know much about her, except that she was an environmental scientist and she was dating a new deputy with the sheriff's department.

"That was an amazing rescue tonight," he said.

"I'm in awe of people like Sheri and Ryan, who make those dangerous climbs," Grace said. "And in the dark. I'm literally just learning the ropes, and I don't ever think I'll be that skilled and confident."

"How did you get involved with search and rescue?" he asked.

"I like helping others and making a difference." She flashed a smile. "And it gets me out of my own head. I could easily turn into a hermit if I didn't force myself to get out and be part of the community. This is a good way to do that. And I'm learning new skills, getting into shape—I love it. Even when the rescues are hard or dangerous. It's all important, and how often do any of us get to do something that's really important?"

"I guess you're right." He had joined search and rescue because he remembered how hard they had worked to help find Valerie. Even though they hadn't succeeded, the memory of those dedicated volunteers had stuck with him. And though he had never mentioned this when he applied to be a volunteer, he had hoped that time spent in remote locations in the mountains might lead to him uncovering a clue about what had happened to Valerie. He had imagined that would mean finding her body, or at least something that had belonged to her. That hadn't happened, but until the mystery of her disappearance was solved, he would never let go of the hope of finding a solution.

"The new girl seems really nice," Grace said.

"Bethany? Yeah, she's nice."

"She's shy, like me, but I can tell she's trying to come out of her shell."

"I guess so." Maybe he was reading too much into her attention to him. Some people were just friendly.

"Hey, what is that all over your truck?"

Grace's steps faltered, then stopped. Vince stopped also, and stared at his truck. The moon had risen, and even in that silvery light, he could tell something was wrong with the paint job on the truck. It was too splotchy. He broke into a run and stopped when his boots crunched on broken glass. Every window in the truck was shattered. The windshield was still holding together, though a spiderweb of cracks spread out from a spot centered over the driver's side.

"Is that red paint?" Grace spoke from beside him.

Vince crunched toward the truck until he could touch the dark stain across the hood. His finger came away red and sticky. He stared, realizing something was scrawled amid the broken lines of the windshield glass—messy words in the same red paint.

YOU THOUGHT I WAS DEAD, DIDN'T YOU?

"What's that at the bottom?" Caleb had joined Vince and Grace. "It looks like a check mark."

"It's not a check mark," Vince said. He stared at the two slashes of paint meeting at the bottom. "It's a *V*." *V* for *Valerie*.

Chapter Nine

Tammy headed back down the hill toward her car. She searched groups of people she passed, hoping to spot Vince. She would say hello, and they could make small talk about the accident. Maybe they could firm up dinner plans.

A crowd had gathered on the side of the road up ahead. Curious, Tammy pushed through the clot of people and was startled to see Vince standing in front of his truck. Several people were shining flashlights on the vehicle, revealing a broken window and splashes of red paint. Tammy stared at the message on the windshield: YOU THOUGHT I WAS DEAD, DIDN'T YOU? V.

Deputy Shane Ellis, along with Colorado State Patrol Officer Ryder Stewart, moved in alongside Vince and began talking to him. Tammy snapped off a few photographs of the scene, then joined them. "Hello, Vince," she said during a lull in the conversation.

"Hey, Tammy." He resumed staring at his truck. "I can't believe this happened."

Tammy turned to Shane. "Who did this?" she asked.

"We haven't found anyone who saw anything," Shane said.

"Everyone was focused on the accident, and it was dark," Ryder said. "The road was closed, and there weren't a lot of people along this stretch where the volunteers parked their cars. We've got a shoe impression where a person stepped in the paint. It may have been the perpetrator, or maybe someone who was trying to get a closer look." He studied Tammy's tennis shoes. "The print is about your size."

"No paint on me or my shoes." She extended her leg so he could examine the sole of first one shoe, then the other. "So you think a woman did this?"

"It's a possibility," Ryder said. "But only *one* possibility."

"Someone could have parked on the other side of the closure and hiked up the road like I did," she said. "If they waited until everyone was up at the accident site, maybe when the helicopter arrived and was making a lot of noise and attracting everyone's attention. Then they smashed the windows, wrote the message and tossed the paint, and left before anyone saw them."

"That could be how it happened," Ryder said. "Do you know something about it?"

"I got to the accident site a few minutes before the helicopter arrived," she said. "While I was walking up the road, a woman ran past me. I didn't get a good look, but I'm pretty sure it was a woman—slender and not too tall, dressed in dark clothing. I noticed her because she was running—and away from the accident, not toward it like everyone else."

Vince was focused on her now. "What color hair did she have? Did you get a look at her face?"

"No. I was focused on getting to the accident scene. And she was moving pretty fast."

"Did you see where she went?" Shane asked.

"No, I didn't," she admitted.

"The message is signed *V*," Vince said.

"Do you think it's Valerie?" Tammy asked.

"I don't know what to think," he admitted.

"Both of you need to come down to the department and

give a statement," Shane said. "Meanwhile, we'll go over the truck for evidence."

"I can give you a ride to town," Tammy said.

Vince looked glum. "Why would anyone go after my truck? And why the cryptic message?"

"I don't know," Tammy said. "Maybe the sheriff can figure something out." She didn't believe that. Whoever was pretending to be Valerie, she hadn't provided them with evidence of her motive, other than to harass Vince. "Do you have an ex who is angry with you? If she knows about Valerie, she might be hiding behind the name as a way of unsettling you."

"It's unsettling, all right. But no, I don't have any exes, angry or otherwise. I told you, I'm not the best at relationships."

She wanted to reassure him that he was just fine, that no one was an expert at these things, but what did she know? Better to focus on being his friend. If something more developed, that would be good, but better not to force it.

VINCE SLID INTO the passenger seat of Tammy's Subaru, the image of his vandalized truck still fixed in his mind. *You thought I was dead, didn't you?* Of course he thought Valerie was dead. Hundreds of people had searched for her immediately after she went missing, and they hadn't found one clue as to what happened to her. No one had heard from her in fifteen years. She had disappeared in the high mountains, where people died in accidents every year. One wrong step or a slip could send a person plummeting off a cliff or into a deep fissure in the rocks, and no one would ever see them again.

Whoever was doing this couldn't be Valerie. She would have no reason to taunt him this way. The real Valerie would be happy to see him again.

But a scammer would demand money, and that hadn't happened yet.

Which left someone who was doing this in order to torture Vince and his family. A person who enjoyed making other people suffer. Was it someone he knew or a stranger who had read the article in the *Examiner* and decided to focus on him? "Has anyone contacted the paper about the article you wrote?" he asked Tammy.

"What do you mean by *contact*?" she asked. "A few people complimented me on the article. And some people asked what else I had planned for the series."

"I'm thinking maybe someone saw the article and fixated on it as a way to harass me," he said. "I've heard of people who enjoy psychologically torturing others. Some of the calls my parents received soon after Valerie disappeared were made by people like that. They would say things like 'Your daughter is being tortured, and you'll never see her again.'"

"That's so cruel," she said.

"It is. I'm trying to figure out if the person who sent that postcard and vandalized my car is like that. They've decided for whatever reason to target me, and Valerie's story is a convenient one to hide behind." The idea made sense—more sense than the possibility that Valerie had suddenly shown up again after all these years.

"You should tell the sheriff that," she said. "There might even be someone who contacted your parents before who has resurfaced."

At the sheriff's department, Tammy left with Shane to give her statement while Jake Gwynn escorted Vince to an interview room. They had scarcely settled into chairs across from each other when Travis entered. "I might have a few questions after you've given your statement to Jake about what happened tonight."

Vince took him through the events of the evening, from when he had first parked his truck on the side of the closed highway to his arrival back there two hours later, and the vandalism he had seen. "You're sure the note was signed *V*?" Jake asked. "It couldn't have been some random paint drip?"

Vince thought back to the message on the windshield. "I'm pretty sure it was *V*," he said.

"Do you know who *V* might be?" Jake asked.

"I think it's someone who is trying to make me think the message was written by my sister, Valerie." Vince looked to Travis. "Maybe the same person who sent that postcard."

"You don't believe this really is Valerie?" Travis asked.

"How could it be? If she's still alive, why haven't we heard anything for fifteen years? And if she was kidnapped and suddenly escaped, you'd think she'd be thrilled to see us again. She wouldn't hide and try to frighten us."

Travis scooted his chair closer and looked Vince in the eye. "Did you have anything to do with your sister's disappearance?"

"What? No!"

"Is it possible Valerie might have thought you had something to do with the accident or whatever happened that day?" Travis continued. "Maybe you were playing and she slipped and fell, and you were too afraid to tell anyone. Or you dared her to do something and she took the dare and was hurt."

"No! I was in the tent, asleep, when she disappeared. I saw her leave the tent, then fell back asleep. By the time I woke up, my parents were already searching."

Travis's expression gave nothing away. Vince glared at him. "Do you think this is Valerie? And that she's exacting revenge for something I did to her?"

"I think it's always a good idea to look at every possibility," Travis said.

"If this is my sister, where has she been all this time? And why couldn't hundreds of people searching for her find any trace after that day?"

"I don't know," Travis said. "But I'm doing my best to find out. Is there anything else about tonight, or about the postcard or the message left on your truck, that makes you think of anything or anyone?"

"No. I've gone over and over it in my head, and I can't think of anything, except that this is another scammer or one of those people who likes to torture others. My parents got calls like that after Valerie disappeared. Is it possible this is one of those people and the article in the *Examiner* shifted their focus to me?"

"Do you know the names of any of those people?" Travis asked.

"I don't think so, but I'll ask my parents." Although that would mean involving them in this, and he had been hoping to avoid that. "Maybe you have something in your files on the case," he said.

"I haven't found anything, but I promise I'll take a look." Travis stood. "Jake will print your statement and you can sign it, then you're free to go. Call us in a day or two, and we'll let you know when you can have your truck."

"I hate to think how much it's going to cost to restore the truck," he said.

Travis didn't comment on this, merely said good-night and left the room. Vince waited for the printout of his statement, read over it and then dashed off his signature. It wasn't until he was walking down the hall that he wondered how he was going to get to his condo. But when he stepped into the lobby, Tammy rose from a chair by the door. "I waited to give you a ride home," she said.

"Thanks."

He didn't say anything else until they were seated in her car. "Are you going to write about my truck being vandalized for the paper?" he asked.

"I don't know," she said. "I have to work on the story about the truck accident and the rescue." She glanced at him, then back at the road. "Why?"

"I'd rather you didn't," he said. "I don't want to upset my parents, but most of all, I don't want to give whoever this is more attention."

"If we do run anything, it's most likely to be a line item in the sheriff's report. But it isn't my decision to make. That would be up to my editor."

"You don't have to give him the photos you took," he said.

"No, I don't." She fell silent, and he worried he had hurt her feelings.

"I'm not trying to tell you how to do your job," he added. "And I'm grateful for all the help you've given me. I'm just trying to sort out how to handle all of this."

"I know." She turned into the parking area for his condo and pulled into an empty space. She unfastened her seat belt but kept the engine running. "I'm sorry about your truck," she said. "That has to feel like a personal attack."

"It does," he agreed. "That message—'You thought I was dead, didn't you?' As if I betrayed my sister by believing she was no longer alive."

"Even though a lot of people share that assumption."

"I'm angry that I'm letting some sick person get to me this way," he said.

"Don't beat yourself up for being human." She reached over and took his hand. Her skin was cool and smooth, her touch firm and comforting. "I wish I could do more to help."

"You're doing a lot just being here." He turned toward

her, and she surprised him by leaning over and pressing her lips to his.

He leaned into the kiss, pulled by attraction and need. Then, just as suddenly, she pulled away. The kiss was brief, but the impression of it lingered. She gave a nervous laugh and didn't meet his gaze. "Call me if you need anything else," she said, and fastened her seat belt.

That seemed the definite signal for him to leave. "I will," he said. "And thanks for everything."

He got out of the car and forced himself to walk up to his condo without looking back. He was relieved to find no nasty notes on his door. He sank onto the couch and leaned forward, elbows on knees and head in his hand. His lips still tingled from that kiss. He liked Tammy. He liked being with her. He was attracted to her, and it would be fun to explore that attraction. But was now the time to get involved with anyone, with everything stirred up over Valerie?

Though, when he looked at his life closely, he recognized that Valerie had been his excuse for not getting serious about anyone all his life. Since his twin had vanished all those years ago, he had grown used to being alone. Valerie wasn't half of him, but she was part of him. She was part of his life even though she was no longer in it, and he didn't know how to explain that to someone else. Valerie wasn't dead, but she would never be truly gone either. He had always wondered if finding her body would make it easier to finally lay her to rest.

Instead, he was grappling with someone who claimed his sister was still alive and wasn't happy with him. Valerie was still taking up too much room in his head and his life to make it possible to be there for someone else.

Chapter Ten

Wednesday morning, Tammy sat at her desk in the office of the *Eagle Mountain Examiner*, reviewing the photos she had taken the night before. She was supposed to be selecting the image from the rescue to run with the story she had already turned in. But her attention kept returning to the shots she had taken of Vince's vandalized car. *You thought I was dead, didn't you?* And that slash of a *V* beneath. If it was possible for a painted message to look angry, this one did.

She replayed those few seconds when the figure had run past her in the dark—slender body, long hair—and something about the way they moved had made Tammy certain it was a woman. Who would be running away from the accident, unless it was the person who had vandalized Vince's car?

Tammy had arrived at the scene after all the rescue personnel were in place. Law enforcement was either stationed at the highway barricade or near the accident site. Could one of them have seen the same fleeing woman?

She stood and walked to the open door of Russ's office. He was hunched over his desk, frowning at his computer monitor, but looked up at her approach. "What?" he asked.

"I'm going out to do background interviews for a story I'm working on," she said.

"Go." He waved her away and returned to scowling at the monitor.

She slung her handbag over one shoulder and headed on foot to the sheriff's department. It was the kind of perfect summer day that made tourists congratulate themselves on having chosen such an idyllic spot for a vacation—sunny but not hot, with cloudless turquoise skies and blooming flowers everywhere you looked.

The atmosphere was less sunny in the lobby of the sheriff's department. Office Manager Adelaide Kinkaid looked up from her command center at the front desk, her expression stern. "What can I do for you, Ms. Patterson?" she asked.

"I'd like to speak to the sheriff," Tammy said.

"Sheriff Walker does not have time to speak with the press," Adelaide said, her response to every request Tammy had ever made to speak with the sheriff.

"Then I need to speak with one of the deputies who responded to the accident at Carson Canyon last night."

Adelaide's eyes narrowed. "What do you need to know?"

"I need to clarify a couple of facts for the article I wrote." Pause, and an earnest expression. "I would hate to get anything wrong."

Adelaide's frown tightened, but after a few seconds, she picked up the phone and asked a deputy to come to the lobby to speak with "the reporter from the *Examiner*." As if everyone in town didn't already know Tammy was the sole reporter—well, except for the high school student who covered school sports each year, and Russ, who did write his share of news stories.

Deputy Jamie Douglas smiled when she saw Tammy. Tammy returned the smile. She and Jamie were friends, and she didn't have to worry about her friend being evasive. Jamie glanced at Adelaide. "Come on back, and we'll talk at my desk," she said.

As they walked down the hallway to the crowded bullpen where Jamie shared a desk with other deputies, the two friends exchanged the usual pleasantries. "How is Olivia?" Tammy asked.

"We think she's going to start crawling any minute now," Jamie said of her three-month old daughter. "And she's growing like crazy. Nate says she's going to be tall like him, but I think it's too soon to tell." They arrived at Jamie's desk. "Adelaide said you had some questions about the accident last night?"

"Yes. I wanted to know who was working the barricade where they closed the highway."

"I was."

"Did anyone try to get past you? On foot, maybe?"

"No. You and the rescue personnel are the only people we let through."

Maybe the woman she had seen had slipped through before the barricade went up. "Did you see anyone leaving the area?" Tammy asked. "Anyone you didn't recognize, or who wasn't authorized to be there?"

"No. Why?"

She explained about the running woman who had passed her as she hiked up the hill.

"I didn't see anyone like that," Jamie said. She looked over Tammy's shoulder. "Dwight, come here a minute."

Deputy Dwight Preston joined them. "Hi, Tammy."

"Dwight, did you see anyone come or go past the barricade last night who you didn't know? Anyone who wasn't with search and rescue or highway patrol?"

"There was the other reporter," he said.

"What other reporter?" Tammy asked.

"With the *Junction Sentinel*. She said the couple in the truck were from Junction, and she was covering the story."

Tammy's heart raced. "What did she look like?"

"About your height. Slender. She was wearing dark jeans and a dark shirt and a baseball cap. I couldn't see her hair."

"Did she give a name?" Jamie asked.

"No. She just said she was a reporter with the *Sentinel*. She had a camera and a notebook, so I let her through."

"Were the couple in the truck from Junction?" Tammy asked.

Jamie and Dwight looked at each other. "I'll check," Jamie said, and turned to her computer.

"Is something wrong?" Dwight asked.

Tammy explained about the running woman. "It sounds like it could have been the same woman," Dwight said. "Maybe she was in a hurry to get back to town and file her story."

Jamie looked up. "The couple was from North Carolina," she said.

Tammy thanked them and hurried back to the newspaper office. From there, she telephoned the Junction paper and asked for her friend, Tyler Frazier. "Hey, Tammy!" he greeted her. "This is a nice surprise."

"Hey, Tyler. I'm trying to locate a reporter there at the paper. She was here in Eagle Mountain last night, covering an accident we had where a couple's truck went off the road and over a cliff."

"Sounds like a wild story, but I don't think we would have sent a reporter to cover it," he said. "That's pretty far out of our coverage area."

"Would you mind checking for me?"

"Okay. Hold on a second."

He put her on Hold. A song that was popular when her parents were teenagers came on, and Tammy hummed along as she studied the photos of the vandalized truck once more. She had taken one of the red footprint, left when someone—

the vandal?—had stepped in the red paint. Red like blood. She shivered at the thought.

Tyler came back on the line. "No one here went down to Eagle Mountain yesterday to cover an accident or anything else," he said. "What did this reporter look like?"

"Female, young, slender, about my height. Maybe with long hair." The woman who had run past her had had long hair.

"That doesn't sound like anyone we have on staff," Tyler said. "Sorry I can't help you."

She hung up. Someone had posed as a reporter in order to get past the highway barrier. Had she done so specifically to get to Vince's truck? But why? Why target him?

The phone rang, the screen showing a familiar name. "Hello, Mitch," she said.

"Come have lunch with me," Mitch said.

She started to tell him she was too busy. Truthfully, she wasn't in the mood to socialize, even with Mitch.

"Please. Elisabeth will be there, and I want you to meet her."

"All right." She couldn't pass up the chance to meet the woman who had captivated her brother.

"Meet us at the Rib Shack at twelve thirty."

When she arrived at the barbecue stand near the river, she spotted Mitch already in line. Next to him was a slender, dark-haired woman about her height, whom he introduced as Elisabeth. The woman's smile was warm, her handshake firm. "It's nice to meet you," she said.

"It's good to meet you too," Tammy said. "And welcome to Eagle Mountain. Mitch tells me you're new in town."

"Yes. He's been helping me get settled." She gave Mitch an adoring smile, which he returned. Tammy had never seen her brother this besotted. Why was that unsettling?

"What brought you to Eagle Mountain?" Tammy asked. "We're not exactly on the beaten path."

"I had a friend who used to live here," she said. "She raved about how beautiful it is, and I can't say she was wrong."

It was their turn to order. When they had collected their food, they carried it to a picnic table in the shade of a towering blue spruce. Elisabeth and Mitch settled across from Tammy, sitting so close their shoulders touched.

"Elisabeth, where are you from?" Tammy asked.

"Nebraska."

"Oh, do you have family there?"

Elisabeth's expression saddened. Something about her was familiar to Tammy, but she couldn't place her. "Not anymore. My father passed away recently, and I'm all alone."

"I'm sorry to hear that. You don't have other family?"

"No one close, no." She glanced at Mitch. "Not everyone is lucky enough to have a close sibling."

"Are you in Eagle Mountain for long?" Tammy asked.

"I hope so." She beamed at Mitch, and he beamed back. Why did this set Tammy's teeth on edge? Was she jealous that Mitch was happy and she wasn't? No. She wasn't like that. And Elisabeth seemed perfectly nice.

"Mitch tells me you're a reporter," Elisabeth said, her attention on Tammy once more. "That must be such interesting work."

"It is."

"What are some of the stories you've covered?" She propped her chin on her hand, eyes laser-focused on Tammy.

Tammy shifted, uncomfortable under that intense gaze. "Last night I covered an accident. A truck went off the road and plunged over a cliff, but it was caught halfway down on a boulder. Search and rescue had to make a dangerous climb down to stabilize the truck and retrieve the accident victims."

"That certainly sounds dramatic," Elisabeth said.

"It was." She studied the other woman more closely. "You weren't up there near the accident scene last night, were you?"

"Who, me?" Elisabeth looked amused. "Why would you think that?"

"I thought I saw you up there." Tammy couldn't be sure, but Elisabeth might have been the figure who ran by her.

Elisabeth chuckled. "It wasn't me." She leaned into Mitch. "I was otherwise occupied."

"Elisabeth was with me last night," Mitch said. He put his arm around her shoulders.

"It must have been someone else, then." Tammy focused on her lunch, though she scarcely tasted the spicy barbecue.

"You wrote that article about the little girl who disappeared, didn't you?" Elisabeth said.

"Yes."

Elisabeth glanced at Mitch. "I read it when I first got to town. It's hard to believe anyone could just vanish that way."

"It happens more often than you would think," Mitch said. "There's a lot of hazardous country. It's easy to get lost or have an accident."

"I would think parents of a child would keep a closer eye on them." Elisabeth popped a french fry into her mouth.

"Apparently, Valerie slipped out of the tent early in the morning, before the rest of the family was awake," Tammy said.

"Well, the parents would say that if they wanted to cover up their own guilt, wouldn't they?"

Before Tammy could question this odd assertion, another local real estate agent stopped by their table to say hello. Mitch introduced Elisabeth, who smiled warmly and leaned closer to Mitch.

When the other man left, Tammy gathered up the remains of her lunch. "I'd better get back to work," she said. "It was nice meeting you, Elisabeth."

"You too." Elisabeth linked her arm with Mitch's. "I'm sure we're going to be seeing a lot more of each other."

Tammy took the longest route back to the newspaper office, trying to walk off her mixed emotions about her brother's newest girlfriend. Was it the swiftness with which the relationship had progressed that unsettled her? She clearly wasn't the woman who had impersonated a reporter from Junction last night, or the person who had run past Tammy and maybe vandalized Vince's car. Tammy hadn't dared press for more details, but her brother's smug expression seemed to imply that he and Elisabeth had spent the entire night together.

Back at the office, she got to work on an article summarizing the most recent town council meeting and rewriting a press release from a local charitable organization.

Hours later, she was gathering her things to leave when the receptionist, Micki, a high school student who worked from one to six most afternoons, came over to her desk. "Someone just put this through the mail slot," she said. "It's addressed to you."

Tammy accepted the envelope and stared at her name in crooked block print across the front. The printing looked familiar. She worked her thumb beneath the flap and teased it open. The message inside was typed.

Dear Tammy
As a reporter, I'm sure you're interested in the truth. I read the article you wrote about the disappearance of Valerie Shepherd and feel the need to set a few things straight.

Despite what the Shepherds have told everyone for years, Valerie did not simply wander off. Her parents—and her brother, Vince—deliberately left her in those mountains to die. That was the whole reason they even went into the mountains that weekend. The family had other things to do that weekend, but Mr. Shepherd insisted they had to go. He couldn't wait to get rid of the difficult child in the family. I guess he thought life would be easier with only Vince, his perfect son, to contend with. If not for the kindness of a stranger who found her, Valerie would have perished. The truth is, her family didn't want her anymore. Fortunately, she ended up with someone who did want her.

This is the truth you need to let the public know about.

V.

Chapter Eleven

Vince read the letter through twice, heart hammering wildly. "It's not true," he said. "My parents and I didn't abandon Valerie. My parents were crushed by her disappearance. We've never stopped hoping she would be found."

"Why would anyone write these accusations?" Sheriff Walker tapped the corner of the letter, which was laid out on the table in the interview room at the sheriff's department. After Tammy had telephoned to tell him about the note, Vince had agreed to meet her at the sheriff's office, a place that was becoming all-too familiar to him after his recent visits. Travis sat on one side of the table, his brother, Sergeant Gage Walker, standing behind him. Vince and Tammy sat side by side across from him, not touching, but close enough that he could sense the rise and fall of her breath. This note had clearly unnerved her, and seeing her so upset had shaken him.

He forced his attention back to the sheriff's question. "I don't know." He stared at the single *V* typed at the bottom of the letter.

"It sounds to me like someone's pretending to be Valerie," Tammy said.

"It's signed the same way as the message left on my truck's windshield," Vince said.

"Did your sister sign her name that way?" Travis asked. "A single *V*?"

"No. But we were only ten when she disappeared." He tried to think but drew a blank. "I can't say I'd ever seen her sign anything."

"The letter writer refers to Valerie in the third person," Tammy said. "She doesn't say 'I did not simply wander off,' but '*Valerie* did not simply wander off.'" She shrugged. "I don't know if that's significant. It's just an observation."

"Maybe she likes to refer to herself in the third person," Travis said.

"Or maybe this isn't Valerie." Vince shook his head. "Of course it isn't Valerie."

Gage spoke for the first time. "Why do you say that?"

"Because even if Valerie is alive, she has no reason to want to hurt me. We were twins." He looked down at the table and swallowed past a lump in his throat. "Losing her was like losing part of myself."

"She's been gone a long time," Gage said. "Maybe she thinks you didn't do enough to find her. Or she blames you for whatever happened to her."

"But what could have happened to her?" Vince asked.

Gage and Travis exchanged a glance, though he couldn't read the meaning behind that look. It was the kind of coded expression couples or siblings shared—the kind of communication he and Valerie had once enjoyed. "At the time your sister disappeared, both you and your parents mentioned another camper in the area," Travis said.

"Valerie said there was a man camped near us," Vince said. "I never saw him, and when we searched the area for him, we never saw any sign of him."

"Was it like her to make things up?" Travis asked.

"No. I believed there was a camper and he left early."

"Maybe he took Valerie with him when he left," Gage said.

"I know my parents thought so," Vince said. "They urged law enforcement to look for the man, and I believe they tried to find him. But no one else reported seeing him, and we didn't have much to go on—just a man with a blue tent."

Tammy leaned forward, her expression eager. "Do you think Valerie was kidnapped by this man and, after fifteen years, managed to escape and come looking for her family?" she asked.

"It's one possibility," Travis said. "Though that's not to go any further than this room."

Tammy shrank back at his stern look. "Yes, sir," she said.

Travis slid the letter into an evidence bag. "Or maybe this is a hoax." He regarded Vince for a long moment. Vince tried to remain still, to not reveal how unsettled the sheriff's scrutiny made him. "Are you sure you can't think of anyone who might want to harass you?" Travis asked. "An ex–romantic partner or someone you worked with? A former neighbor or classmate? Maybe another family member?"

"No one," Vince said.

"You can't think of anyone who has any reason to be unhappy with you?" Gage asked.

Vince shrugged. "No. I guess I'm not the kind of guy to upset people." The truth was, he seldom got close enough to anyone to upset them—or to make much of an impression at all. He had friends. He had dated several women. But he couldn't say any of those relationships had the depth he thought was required to end up with someone wanting to wreck his truck—or his life.

Travis stood and Gage moved away from the wall. "Those are all my questions for now," the sheriff said.

Vince followed Tammy out of the interview room, down the hall and onto the sidewalk. She stopped at the corner and hugged her arms across her chest. "That was frustrating," she said. "I was hoping the sheriff would have more answers."

"Do you think Valerie could be the one doing this?" he asked. "Sending those notes and vandalizing my truck? Has she been alive all these years and we didn't know?"

Tammy angled toward him, her expression soft with concern. "There have been other cases, of children who were abducted and turned up alive years later," she said.

"Then why not just contact me and tell me the truth?" Frustration made knots in his gut. "Why attack my truck and accuse me of helping to get rid of her?"

"It does feel like there's a lot of animosity in those letters—and what was done to your truck..." Tammy rubbed her hands up and down her arms as if she was cold.

It did. The idea that his sister—his twin whom he had loved without even having to think about it—would *hate* him this way felt dark and ugly.

They resumed walking, he assumed back toward the newspaper office. This time of day, the sidewalks were full of tourists and locals, running errands or visiting the shops and restaurants. He and Tammy had to walk close together, shoulders bumping frequently, in order to have a conversation. "What was Valerie like as a girl?" Tammy asked. "I mean, her temperament and attitudes? Was she like you or the opposite? Or somewhere in-between?"

He considered the question. Valerie had been such an essential part of his life that he had taken for granted she would always be there—until she wasn't. And at ten years old, he hadn't spent much time thinking about how other people felt or how they were different from him. But he had had a lot of time since then to examine everything he knew about his sister. "Valerie was more outgoing than I was," he said. "More daring. She would talk to strangers in public or wander off on her own when we were in the park or out shopping."

"Then she wouldn't have been afraid, necessarily, of a stranger who approached her?" Tammy asked.

"No. I mean, our parents and teachers had talked to us about stranger danger. Valerie was smart. I don't think she would have gotten into a car with someone she didn't know. But if a person struck up a conversation with her, she would have been friendly. And she liked attention. I guess she was kind of a show-off."

"Did that bother you when you were a boy? That she tried to get attention?"

"No. I didn't care. I wasn't interested in having people pay attention to me."

"Did she have a temper? Was she quick to anger or to take offense?"

"Oh yeah." He remembered. "She would get so mad sometimes. Her face would turn red, and she would stomp her foot." He almost smiled, picturing her rage over not being allowed to do something she wanted to do. "It's not fair!" she had howled, furious about not getting her way.

"But she could be sweet too," he said. "That weekend of the camping trip, I was upset about missing a friend's birthday party. Valerie tried to make me feel better. She even told my dad she thought I should be allowed to go to the party. And though she teased me about being afraid of things she wasn't—spiders and steep mountain bike tracks and things like that—she was never too hard on me."

"The two of you were close, then?"

He shrugged. "We were twins. And we didn't have any other siblings or cousins who lived nearby. The two of us were kind of a team."

"It must have been hard for you when she disappeared."

"For a long time, it didn't feel real," he said. "I kept think-ing the door would open and she would be there, laughing and telling us all it had been a joke, that she had merely been hiding."

"Cruel joke," Tammy said. "Would she have done some-thing like that?"

"Maybe," he said. "It would have been better than the truth—that we never knew what happened to her."

But what if the person who was harassing him now did turn out to be Valerie? Would that be worse than believing she had died? He couldn't wrap his head around the answer. "I'd like to know what happened to her," he said. "And I want whoever is sending these letters and whoever attacked my truck to be found and stopped."

"I want that too," Tammy said. She rested her hand on his shoulder. "And I'll do everything I can to help you."

It was the kind of thing any person might say, but he could sense the sincerity behind her words. She cared. The idea touched him—and unsettled him too. He had spent years keeping his distance from people. If you didn't get too close to people, you wouldn't be too hurt when they left you. He understood that not everyone wanted to live that way, but it had worked for him so far. Why should he change now just because one curly-haired reporter was getting under his skin?

Fifteen years ago

"It's MY TURN to hide. You have to find me!" Before Vince could protest, Valerie slapped his shoulder and ran away.

Annoyed, he closed his eyes and began to count. "One, two, three…"

He hated when it was his turn to find Valerie. She never failed to choose the best hiding spots. Impossible spots, like the gap between the cushions and the underside of their hide-a-bed sofa in the den, or in the rafters of the garage. He could spend hours searching for her with no luck, except he often gave up long before then.

Not that it was better when it was his turn to hide. She always found him, usually within ten minutes. Then she would crow about how terrible he was at this game. Which was why he never wanted to play. But today he had made the mistake of promising to play whatever Valerie wanted, never thinking she would choose hide-and-seek on such a hot afternoon. It had to be near ninety degrees out, and the sun was beating down. Maybe that wasn't hot to people like his aunt and uncle from Texas, but here in the mountains, with no air-conditioning in their house, ninety degrees was sweltering.

He reached fifty and decided that was enough. He was supposed to count to one hundred, but with Valerie, he needed any advantage he could grab. He opened his eyes and looked around, searching for any clue as to which direction she had run. He didn't see any footprints in the rocks and grass that made up the empty lot behind their house where they were playing. No flash of the bright red T-shirt she was wearing. The shed door wasn't ajar. Would she hide inside one of the parked cars?

He hurried to his mom's Chevy and opened the rear door. A blast of heat pushed him back. Valerie had better not be in there. She'd roast. He forced himself to stick his head inside and look around, but no Valerie.

No Valerie in the shed either, or behind any of the trees or bigger boulders that ringed the lot. Their rule was that they had to stay within the lot, which was bordered on two sides by wooden fencing. The back side gave way to a steep drop-off. Vince approached this and looked over. It would be just like Valerie to slide down there, thinking it would be a stealthy hiding place, and not be able to get back up. But there was nothing in the gully below but more trees and rocks.

He turned around and faced the house. He hadn't heard a door open or close, but Valerie might have managed to slip inside if she had been quiet. She was good at stealth. Better than he was. He was going through another growth spurt, and everything he did was clumsy. Squinting in the bright sunlight, he moved toward the house. He approached the back door, then looked under the steps. There was a shadowed hollow there where Vince had hidden once. It had taken Valerie over fifteen minutes to find him that time. She had even said it was a good hiding place.

But she hadn't decided to use it this time. He moved along the house, looking behind the lilac bushes, their blooms spent brown twigs now.

Something scrabbled in the loose mulch behind him, and he whirled, heart pounding. He stared at the ground beneath the lilacs. What was down there? He didn't see anything, but something had made that noise. "Valerie?" he asked, tentative.

Fingers gripped his ankle, hard, and yanked. Vince screamed and staggered back, arms flailing. Raucous laughter brought him up short.

Valerie, cobwebs draped across her hair like old lace and a smudge of dirt across one cheek, crawled out from beneath the porch. "Oh my gosh, that was great!" she shrieked, doubled over with laughter. "You screamed like a little girl!"

"You're supposed to be hiding, not attacking me!" he yelled.

"You walked right past me!" she said. "I couldn't resist. Your ankle was right there!"

He stared at the gap in the foundation she had squeezed into. "You have spiderwebs in your hair," he said.

She swept her fingers through her wavy locks, and the sticky webbing clung to them. "There are spiders under there too," she said.

He shuddered. "That's disgusting."

"No it's not. I'm not afraid of a few bugs." She lifted her chin. "I'm not afraid of anything."

Vince envied his sister's fearlessness. He was afraid of so many things—spiders and falling, not catching a fly ball in Little League, failing a math test and being stuck in fourth grade forever. "I bet you're afraid of dying," he said. "Everyone is afraid of that. Even adults."

Valerie shrugged. "I'm not."

"Liar."

She leaned forward and slapped his shoulder. "Your turn to hide. And pick a good place." Then she closed her eyes and started counting out loud. "One, two, three…"

Vince ran. He thought about leaving the yard and heading down the street to his friend Brett's house. That would make Valerie mad, but she'd either tell their mom—in which case, Vince would end up grounded—or she wouldn't tell anyone, but would exact her own revenge, like putting ants in his underwear drawer or putting dog poop in his bed. She had done both of those things before, and Vince had ended up punished when his mother found out. "Valerie wouldn't do something like that," she had said.

And Valerie had played the innocent like a pro, looking at him with wide, hurt eyes. Later, she had sidled up to Vince in the hallway, after his mother had sentenced him to spend an hour every day after school pulling weeds in the flower beds, and whispered, "That'll teach you to try to get the better of me."

Vince ran to the shed and hid behind the lawn mower and paint cans. It wasn't the best hiding place, but it was a good enough spot to sit and think in the moments before Valerie came to find him. He would think about all the things he could do to get back at Valerie, but wouldn't. If she hadn't been his sister, he would have admired her daring instead of being jealous of it. And when it came down to it, he would rather have her on his side than angry with him.

Chapter Twelve

Thursday afternoon, Tammy sat at her desk in the *Examiner* office and paged through the folder of information she had assembled about Valerie Shepherd's disappearance. She had all the original newspaper articles and notes from search and rescue about their role in the hunt for the missing girl, as well as the copy of the sheriff's department file that Travis had given her.

She stopped and reread the initial interview with Victor and Susan Shepherd, then took out a highlighter and ran it over the section where they talked about the camper Valerie claimed to have seen. "Right after we got to camp, Valerie climbed up onto a boulder and said she could see another camper nearby. Someone with a blue dome tent," Susan said. Her husband hadn't even heard this remark. The most information came from Vince, who said Valerie told him she met the man when she went to collect firewood. He had given her wood he had gathered and smiled at her. "She said he had a nice smile," Vince had said.

The sheriff's deputies had asked every person in the area that day if they had seen a lone male camper or backpacker, or one with a little girl who matched Valerie's description. No one had seen him. Appeals to the public who might have seen such a man had yielded nothing.

A man with a nice smile. Had the smile won Valerie over enough that she had gone with him? But where? Vince and his parents swore they had never seen the man, who, if he had been real, had seemingly vanished without a trace. Valerie had risen before the rest of the family and gone out to search for more wood. Had she encountered the man again and he had spirited her away in those early hours before anyone else was on the trail? It was possible, but if that was the case, where had they gone?

She continued reading through the file and came upon a single paragraph from a statement taken from a woman and her boyfriend six months after Valerie's disappearance. They had seen a man with a backpack on a trail near the one the Shepherds had taken, on the day before the Shepherds' camping trip. They described him as medium height and build, brown hair, early to mid-twenties. He wore jeans and a black T-shirt and hiking boots, and had a blue backpack. They hadn't spoken to him and had only come forward after seeing repeated appeals for information about a lone male hiker. "But it was the day before the little girl disappeared, and on a different trail," the woman—Jennifer—had said.

A handwritten note at the bottom of the page stated they were unable to obtain any further information about this man. A second note, in a different colored ink and different handwriting, contained just two words: *probably unrelated.*

That was the last entry in the slim file. Tammy closed the folder and stared into space, hoping for inspiration but finding none. Her stomach growled, and she decided maybe she would think better after lunch.

She walked down the street and was waiting in line for a booth at Kate's Café when a voice behind her said, "Tammy Shepherd? That is you, isn't it?"

She turned to find Elisabeth slipping in behind her.

Tammy glanced past her, expecting to see Mitch. Elisabeth laughed. "Mitch is showing a big ranch over near Delta," she said. "I'm on my own. And it looks like you are too."

The pause after these words was so weighted Tammy felt it pushing against her. "We should have lunch together," she said.

"I'd love that." Elisabeth linked her arm with Tammy's. "It will give us a chance to get to know each other better."

The server arrived to escort them to a booth along the side, and Tammy focused on the menu. But after a few moments, she became aware of Elisabeth studying her. She looked up. "You don't look like Mitch, do you?" Elisabeth said.

"He takes after my dad," Tammy said. "I look more like my mom. Though people say there's a resemblance."

Elisabeth shook her head. "I don't see it. Though maybe some family traits run stronger than that. For instance, my brother and I looked just alike. People thought we were twins."

"Oh. How many siblings do you have?" It seemed a safe enough topic of conversation.

"None. At least, not anymore. He died. My whole family is dead." She smiled, the expression so at odds with her words that Tammy was taken aback.

The server arrived to take their orders, providing a reprieve. Tammy tried to gather her thoughts. When they were alone again, she asked, "Have you been enjoying your time in Eagle Mountain?"

"I have. This morning I went shopping. There's a boutique in the Gold Nugget Hotel. Lucky Strike—do you know it?"

Tammy knew of the boutique, though its prices were beyond what she could manage on her reporter's salary. The styles displayed in the boutique's front windows were more upscale than what she usually wore. She dressed for comfort, ready to race out to the scene of an accident or to interview someone at a construction site or mine. Elisabeth, in her short skirt and heels, looked straight out of a magazine spread. There was no missing the way heads turned to follow her when she crossed a room.

"You're the first newspaper reporter I've ever met," Elisabeth said. "I thought that was one of those jobs that didn't exist anymore."

"People are still interested in the news," Tammy said.

"On television and online, maybe. I thought printed news was going the way of the dinosaurs."

This wasn't the first time Tammy had heard similar statements. "Not our paper," she said. "There's no other source for local news."

"Then you enjoy your job," Elisabeth said.

"Yes." The hours were long and the pay wasn't the best, but reporting was what she had always wanted to do. "The work offers a lot of variety," she said. "And I end up knowing about everything going on."

"What interesting things are going on in Eagle Mountain?"

"Everyone's gearing up for the Fourth of July. It's a big holiday here, for the locals and the tourists. There's a festival and a parade and fireworks."

"It sounds charming."

Tammy couldn't tell if *charming* was a positive or a negative to Elisabeth. "Do they do anything special for the Fourth where you're from?" she asked.

"Different places have fireworks." Elisabeth unrolled her napkin and spread it across her lap. "Mitch told me the two of you have a sibling who died. That's too bad, isn't it?"

Was that a question or an observation? Tammy was saved from having to reply by the arrival of the server with their food. She focused on the food, pondering a way to take the conversation in a less personal direction.

"Do you have a boyfriend?" Elisabeth asked.

Tammy had just taken a large bite of her sandwich and almost choked. She chewed and tried to think of an answer that wouldn't beg elaboration when Elisabeth added, "I saw you with a cute guy outside the sheriff's department. Tall, dark and handsome."

Tammy's face warmed. "That was just a friend."

"Uh-huh." Elisabeth gave her a knowing look. "Does your *friend* have a name?"

"Vince."

Elisabeth poked at her salad with her fork. "What's he like?"

"He's a great guy."

"And you like him a lot. I can tell."

"I do." There was relief in admitting this out loud, an easing of pressure. "But I'm not sure how he feels about me."

"Hmm. Then maybe you should ask him."

Tammy made a face. "I don't want to put him on the spot." And risk scaring him off.

"Okay. Then why not try a little experiment?"

"What do you mean?"

"Turn up the heat and see how he responds."

Tammy flashed back to the one kiss she and Vince had shared. There had been plenty of heat there, but nothing had happened since. "I don't know…"

"Oh, come on," Elisabeth said. "Just try a little seduction. If he goes for it, you'll at least know he's attracted to you physically. That's a place to start."

"Thanks for the suggestion, but that's not my style. Say, how long are you going to be in town? Mitch mentioned you weren't sure when you first moved here."

"I'm still not certain, though this place is growing on me.

And I like your brother. He and I have really clicked." The way she said the words—and the smile that accompanied them—left no doubt that Mitch had responded well to any seduction Elisabeth had directed at him.

But Tammy could have guessed that, seeing how besotted her brother was with this gorgeous woman.

Her phone buzzed, and she slipped it out of her pocket and checked the screen. Where are you? Russ had texted. She imagined the irritation behind the words. The editor wasn't known for his patience. "I have to get back to work," she said. She took out her wallet.

"Oh no." Elisabeth raised a hand. "This is my treat."

"Oh. Thanks. At least let me get the tip."

"It's all taken care of." She pulled out a sleek black credit card.

"Thanks. And I'll, uh, see you soon," she said, and made her exit. No one, she was sure, watched her as she hurried away.

Lunch had been...unsettling. Elisabeth had been friendly and the two women had gotten along, but Tammy realized she still didn't know anything about her brother's new girlfriend—except that startling revelation about a dead brother and two dead parents. Though she had mentioned when they first met that her father had recently died. Elisabeth had deflected any questions about herself, each time turning the conversation back to Tammy.

Maybe Elisabeth was a private person who didn't like to talk about herself. Tammy could respect that. But she wished she and her brother's girlfriend had connected better. Mitch liked her so much that Tammy wanted to like her too.

Some people take longer to warm up to than others, she reminded herself. If Elisabeth did decide to remain in Eagle Mountain, the two of them would have plenty of opportunities to get to know each other better.

VINCE WAS JUST stepping out of the shower Saturday morning when his phone alarmed with an Amber Alert for a missing teen. He was reading through the description of a fifteen-year-old male who had walked out of his family's home the night before when he received the call-out for search and rescue.

Fifteen minutes later, he gathered with other volunteers at search and rescue headquarters. "We're looking for Nicholas Gruber," Danny told the assembled rescuers. "Five feet nine inches tall. Blue eyes. Brown hair. Last seen wearing jeans and a black T-shirt and black running shoes." He lowered the phone from which he had been reading the description. "Apparently, Nicholas had a fight with his mom and dad last night and stormed out. He has done this before, and he always returns in the morning after he's had time to cool off. When he didn't show up this morning, they contacted all his friends, but no one has seen him."

"They must be worried sick," Carrie Andrews said. Vince remembered that she had two children of her own.

"The Grubers live on County Road 7, near Coal Canyon," Danny said. "Nicholas left the house on foot about nine o'clock last night. The sheriff wants to get Anna and her search dog, Jacquie, out there first to see if the dog can pick up the trail. We're on standby to assist in a ground search if they don't find him."

Everyone shifted to look at volunteer Anna Trent and the black standard poodle at her side. The dog, Jacquie, wore a blue vest with *Search Dog* in large white letters on the side. "We're ready," Anna said.

"You and Jacquie can ride with me," Deputy Jake Gwynn said.

He, Anna and the dog left, and the others moved in closer to Danny and Deputy Ryker Vernon. Bethany was there, standing next to Harper, across from Vince. She caught his eye and he nodded, then quickly looked away. He really didn't want to encourage her attention. "We've established a staging area for search volunteers at the lumber mill about a mile from the Grubers' home," Ryker said. "If you'll make your way there, you'll be handy if we need you to help search or if we find Nicholas and he's injured."

While several volunteers piled into the Beast, Vince opted to drive his own vehicle to the lumber mill. Or rather, the car his mother had insisted on lending him when she learned of the damage to his truck. The white Ford Escape was newer and more luxurious than Vince's truck, but he missed his own vehicle, which was still at the sheriff's department impound yard, awaiting the completion of their investigation. Vince wasn't pressuring them to give it back because he doubted he had the funds to pay for the work the truck would need to restore it.

Set back off the road in a stand of tall Douglas fir, the small mill specialized in deck railings, rustic benches and other rough-cut lumber projects. Though the saws were silent today, the smell of fresh sawdust hung in the air. Vince parked beside Ryan Welch's pickup and opened the driver's-side door to let in the scented breeze.

Ryan came over to stand beside Vince and was soon joined by Caleb and Eldon. "I hope Anna and her dog find the kid," Eldon said.

"He's probably just hiding out somewhere," Ryan said. "I did the same thing a couple of times when I was his age—blew up at my parents, then just had to get away for a while."

"Yeah, I guess I did too," Eldon said. "But I'd go stay with my aunt—my dad's younger sister. And she would call my dad and let him know where I was."

"I would go and stay at a friend's house for a couple of days," Caleb said.

The others looked at Vince, who shifted uncomfortably. "I guess I was lucky," he said. "I never fought with my parents." Even if he had, after what had happened with Valerie, he wouldn't have walked out on his mom and dad. It would have worried them too much not to know where he was, even for a few hours.

A loud whistle split the air, and they all turned toward the sound. Danny was standing in the bed of a pickup, motioning for everyone to gather.

"Anna and Jacquie found Nicholas," Danny said when everyone was assembled around the truck. "Apparently, he got disoriented in the darkness and slipped or fell into the canyon. He's okay, except he thinks he broke or sprained his ankle. We're going to have to get him out."

Relief that Nicholas was alive and not in imminent danger energized the group. They gathered equipment and set out to hike to the spot where the teen had fallen. A middle-aged man and woman, both with short hair in shades of brown, were already there. The man lay on his stomach, his attention focused on the boy sprawled fifty yards below. The woman sat beside the man. They both looked up as the rescuers approached. "We're Nicholas's parents," the woman said.

"We're with Eagle Mountain Search and Rescue." Danny introduced himself and shook hands with each of them. "If you could wait back there, away from the edge, we'll have your son with you in no time."

"All right." Mr. Gruber glanced down into the canyon. "He's barely hanging on down there. Are you sure you can get to him without him falling?"

"We'll take care of him." Danny put a hand on the man's shoulder and gently urged him farther back.

The rescuers moved in, the challenge of what they needed to do quickly apparent. The soil along the edge of the canyon was loose, crumbling and raining down onto the boy below repeatedly as they worked. "How are you doing, Nicholas?" Danny called down.

"I'm worried I'm going to fall," came the thin, strained reply. "My ankle's hurt, and every time I try to move, more rock falls."

"Stay still and hang on," Danny instructed. "We need to get things set up here, then we're going to come down to get you."

"Okay. But hurry." Nicholas's voice trembled with fear, but Vince thought he heard determination too.

They were forced to establish an anchor on a tree across the road and ended up using a shovel to dig to more compacted soil before Eldon began the initial descent. Vince helped with the rigging, monitoring the ropes and pulleys and passing whatever equipment Ryan requested as he helped first Eldon, then Danny to descend. Vince found himself holding his breath as the men searched for solid hand- and footholds, the descent slowed by the need to continually reroute to more stable ground. No wonder the kid had fallen.

"I wonder if I'll ever be able to do anything so dangerous."

Vince looked back and found Bethany standing there. She was focused on the scene unfolding below. Then her gaze shifted to him, and the brief, shy smile he had come to associate with her flashed across her face. "I've been doing a little climbing in Caspar Canyon. Sheri and Hannah and some of the others held a kind of clinic for female volunteers."

"That's good," he said.

"At least I know the names of everything now so I can help with the gear."

"You'll get more comfortable the more time you have in." Vince remembered his early days with the group, when he had been overwhelmed by the magnitude of the job they did and uncertain where he fit in with the team.

Bethany was focused on the rescue efforts again, which gave Vince time to study her. She had her dark brown curls pulled back in a low ponytail, and exertion or the breeze in the canyon had reddened her cheeks. She wasn't beautiful, exactly, but cute, in a girl-next-door kind of way. Valerie had been like that. In fact, she and Bethany had the same hair and the same dimple in one cheek. His heart stumbled in its rhythm at the thought, and he stared harder, waiting for some spark of recognition. But nothing happened.

He cleared his throat, and Bethany shifted her attention to him once more. "How long have you been in Eagle Mountain?" he asked.

"Two months."

"Do you have family here? Friends?"

"No. I came for the job at Peak Jeep." She shrugged. "I was ready for a fresh start."

"Why search and rescue?"

"I was looking for a way to get to know more people. And I wanted to do something that would make a difference. Oh, look. They've reached the boy."

Nicholas had been huddled against the ground, one hand over his head to shield him from the worst of the debris that rained down, though more than one fist-sized rock struck his back and many smaller pebbles or dirt clods peppered him.

But now the two rescuers reached him and established themselves on either side of him, and he slumped between them. Eldon fitted the boy with a helmet and harness while Danny assessed his physical condition. "I'm going to fit the ankle with an air boot and give him something for the discomfort," Danny radioed up to Sheri, who was serving as incident commander. "I can't find any other injuries, though he's a little dehydrated from being out here all night. We'll give him some water, and the paramedics can take charge once he's up top."

They sent down more lines, and with a volunteer on either side, Nicholas began the slow ascent. Once he slipped and cried out, but the safety gear arrested his fall, as it was designed to do, and the trio started up again.

Mr. and Mrs. Gruber had gradually moved closer and closer to the edge of the drop-off and were waiting to embrace their wayward son as soon as he stood, somewhat shakily, before them. "I'm sorry," Nicholas said. "I didn't mean to scare you."

His mother wiped at the tears streaming down her son's face, then dashed away her own. "You must have been frightened too, falling in the dark and spending the night not knowing where you were," she said.

"I was worried I'd never get to see you again," Nicholas said, and fought back a sob.

Paramedic Merrily Rayford approached. "We need to get you to the hospital to take care of that ankle," she said. "Mom and Dad can follow in their car."

Vince moved in to help with the ropes while Bethany cleared a path to the waiting ambulance. "That was pretty intense," Vince told Eldon as his fellow volunteer stepped out of his harness.

"Good ending, though," Eldon said.

"Bet he won't be so quick to storm out of the house next time," Ryan said.

"Or maybe his folks will pay a little more attention to how he's feeling," Caleb said.

Vince helped load the equipment, then headed for his car and drove back to his condo. He parked and looked up to find a familiar shapely figure standing in the glow of the light over his front door.

Chapter Thirteen

Vince's heart beat faster as he made his way to the front door. Tammy waved and held up the pizza box she was carrying. "Hey," he said as he drew closer.

"I heard about the rescue," she said. "I thought you might be hungry."

The aroma of pepperoni and cheese made his mouth water. "Thanks," he said, and fished out his keys. "Come on in."

He unlocked the door and she followed him inside. "I hope you don't mind me stopping by," she said.

"Of course not. It's always good to see you."

"I didn't know if you had other plans. After all, it's Saturday night."

"No plans," he said. "Just let me put away this gear."

"I'll meet you in the kitchen."

When he reached the kitchen, she was bent over, sliding the pizza into the oven. She glanced over her shoulder at his approach. "I thought I'd warm it up a little."

"Good idea." She was a little more dressed up than usual, in a pink top that showed a hint of cleavage and a bit of lace. She smelled good too. He wanted to nuzzle her neck and inhale deeply.

He slipped past her and turned away so she wouldn't see the erection this thought had aroused. "How did you hear about the rescue?" he asked as he took plates from the cupboard.

"I have an emergency scanner. It's handy for news stories."

"I'm surprised you weren't there, covering this one."

"Russ lives two houses down, so he volunteered to take it. Didn't you see him there?"

"I wasn't paying attention. I was focused on the rescue."

"Of course. How is the kid who fell?"

"He's going to be fine. And maybe less quick to run away the next time he and his parents don't see eye to eye."

"That's what happened? He ran away?"

"He probably just wanted to take a walk and let off steam, but he got disoriented in the dark and ended up falling into the canyon. The road is pretty narrow, and the soil on the edge was crumbling. It kept collapsing as we were working, trying to set up the rigging to bring him up."

"Sounds like it was a happy ending, though."

"Yeah."

She took the pizza from the oven and carried it to the table. Vince helped himself to a couple of slices. "What happened today made me think about Valerie," he said.

"Oh?"

"This kid was a few hundred yards from his house. When he first fell, he must have shouted for help, but those trees and the dirt and everything absorbs sound. Apparently, no one heard him. And though his parents said they searched for him, they couldn't see him where he was and couldn't hear him. I wonder if something like that happened with Valerie."

"I guess it could have happened that way," she said. "Though you would think, with so many people searching for her, they would have found something."

"Not if she ended up in a deep crevice or a long way from where she fell."

"That's terrible to think about."

It was, but he had tortured himself for years with speculation about his sister's fate. No need to pull Tammy into that. "Did you ever get into fights with your parents and leave the house to cool off when you were a teen?" he asked, thinking about his conversation with his fellow volunteers.

She plucked a piece of pepperoni from the pizza and popped it into her mouth. "I wanted to a few times," she said. "But I never did. My parents had lost one kid. They were terrified of losing another. It made them overprotective, and I chafed against that. But at the same time, I didn't want to hurt them. At least, not any more than they had already been hurt."

"Yeah. It was like that for me too," he said.

She set aside a pizza crust. "I can hardly remember anymore what Mom and Dad were like before my brother died," she said. "Their pain was part of them, like my mom's curly hair or my dad's cleft chin."

"Yeah. I guess you never get over something like that."

"Were your parents overprotective too?"

"Not exactly." It made sense that having lost one child, a parent would hold even more tightly to the offspring left behind. But it hadn't been like that in his house. How to explain it to her without making his parents sound like terrible people? "Losing Valerie was such a blow they kind of, I don't know, checked out for a while," he said. "They couldn't cope. I knew they loved me—and they tried, they really did. But it was like they were in so much pain they didn't have more of themselves to give. I was kind of on my own."

"Oh, Vince."

He winced at the sympathy in her voice. "It was okay. Most of the time, anyway. Birthdays were hard."

"Because it was her birthday too."

"Yeah. When we took that camping trip, my dad tried to make up for me missing my friend's party by saying that when it was my birthday, I could have a sleepover. Not a joint party with Valerie, the way it usually was, but a celebration just for me and my friends. But that never happened."

"Did they not celebrate your birthday at all?" Tammy asked.

"There were always presents and a cake. But there was too much sadness. It was like a weight, pressing us down." He shrugged. "I don't celebrate my birthday anymore. I can't." That day could never be only about him anymore.

"I'm sorry," she said. "But I get it. I always felt like I didn't just lose my brother when Adam died. Our whole family lost itself. We couldn't be the same family we were before, and we never figured out how to completely put ourselves back together."

"You can't," he said. "That one piece is always missing."

They ate in silence for a while, but it wasn't uncomfortable. Tammy was the only person he had ever known who truly understood what growing up had been like for him. And he knew what things had been like for her too. He felt closer to her right now than he had to anyone.

"You look nice tonight," he said.

She smiled, and her cheeks blushed a little pinker. "Thanks." She glanced down at the pink shirt. "I had lunch Thursday with my brother's new girlfriend, Elisabeth. She's always perfectly put together. I guess she inspired me to make a little more effort with my appearance."

"You always look good," he said.

Their eyes met, and in that moment he felt so…whole. As if he didn't need anything else but to be here, right now, with this woman.

They finished eating and carried their dishes in the sink. She started to turn on the water, but he put his hand on her arm. "Don't worry about those now," he said. "Let's go into the living room and talk."

They sat side by side on the sofa, but instead of saying anything, she leaned over and kissed him. Her lips were soft, their gentle pressure making him aware of every sensation firing in his body at her touch. She pressed her palm to his chest, over his heart, every hard beat reverberating through them both.

He pulled her close, clinging to her like a drowning man, a wave of longing almost pulling him under. He kissed her hard, then drew back a little to look at her. She stared back. Was he reading her true feelings in that look or his own emotional turmoil reflected back at him? "I really, really like you," he said.

She looked amused, and slid her hand down his chest to the waistband of his jeans. "I really like you too."

Words failed him as she traced the top of his waistband with one finger. "I want you, Vince," she said.

"Yes." He smothered any reply she might have made with another kiss, and followed eagerly as she lay back and pulled him down with her. He slid one hand beneath her shirt, gliding over the satiny skin of her stomach and up to cup one full breast. He fought the urge to tear at her clothing, wanting to see and feel all of her at once. Only now did he realize how much he had been holding back. "That first day we met, I was attracted to you," he said, nuzzling her neck. "Your perfume drove me wild."

"I don't wear perfume," she said.

"Maybe it's something else, but you smell amazing." He inhaled deeply and smiled. Vanilla, floral and definitely sexy. "Maybe it's just you."

"Mmm." She wrapped both legs around him, pulling him

even closer, and for a long while, conversation ceased as they lost themselves in playful discovery.

Finally, flushed and a little out of breath, she pushed against him. "Why don't we go into the bedroom?" she suggested.

He levered up on his elbows. He must have been crushing her. "Good idea," he said.

"Oh, I'm full of good ideas." The knowing smile that accompanied the words sent a fresh jolt of heat through him. Wanting something this much was exhilarating. And a little terrifying. *You've done this before*, he reminded himself as he took her hand and pulled her toward his bedroom.

That was true, but he wasn't sure getting it right had ever mattered so much.

TAMMY WASN'T A WEEPER. Sappy commercials and sad novels didn't make her tear up the way they did many of her friends. But lying here in Vince's bed had her blinking against a stinging in her eyes. Vince cared so much. He cared about her and how she felt. "Is that good?" he asked as he moved down her naked body. "Do you like that?"

"Everywhere you touch me feels good," she said. "Just keep doing what you're doing. I'll let you know if there's anything I don't like."

But there wasn't anything about him she didn't like— from the sculpted muscles of his arms and shoulders to the strong curve of his thighs, to the smile that pulled at his lips as he traced the lines of her body with his mouth, proof that he liked what he was discovering.

He had taken out a condom without her having to ask, and when they came together, he was gentle, holding back. She stroked his shoulders. "It's okay," she said. "You can't hurt me."

"I don't want to be too rough," he said, his voice ragged.

"You won't be."

He was less careful then, and she was soon caught up in the intensity. There was something erotic about seeing him like this, on the edge of control, and knowing she had brought him to this point. She had never been this aware of her partner's desire in the midst of her own, and that knowledge acted like a multiplier, heightening every sensation. They found a rhythm, hard and deep, and she gave herself up to it, riding the waves of sensation, not even minding as tears slipped out of the corners of her eyes as she reached her climax.

He trembled in her arms, and she held him tightly as he found his own release. They lay together for a long moment, not speaking, his weight heavy but still feeling good.

Finally, he levered off her. "I must be crushing you," he said, and moved to lie beside her.

"No, it was wonderful." She idly stroked his hair. "You're wonderful."

He didn't say *You're wonderful too*, or any clichéd response. Instead, he rested his head in the hollow of her shoulder and his hand across her stomach, cradling her as if she was so precious he couldn't find the words.

"I WISH WE could stay here like this all day," Vince said the next morning after he and Tammy had made love again. They lay in a tangle of sheets, sunlight pouring through the thin sheers over the bedroom window.

"We'd have to send out for food," she said. "And coffee."

He sat up. "I'll make coffee," he said. "And breakfast. But then I have to leave. I promised my dad I'd play golf with him today, and he likes to get an early tee time."

"My mom is making Sunday dinner for my brother and his girlfriend," Tammy said. "I need to be there too."

Vince pulled on his jeans, then looked over his shoulder at her. "I'd rather be with you."

That look—a little possessive, a lot lustful—sent a tremor through her. "I'd rather be with you too," she said. "But family is important."

"Of course it is." He opened a dresser drawer and pulled out a shirt. She began dressing also. Even if he had never put it into words, she figured he felt the same obligation she did. It wasn't enough that they be their parents' children. They had to try to make up for their missing sibling, impossible as that might be.

They parted at his front door with a passionate kiss. "See you later?" he asked.

"For sure."

She had texted her mother the night before to let her know she was spending the night "with a friend" and expected a full interrogation, and maybe a lecture, when she walked in. Instead, the only thing her mother said was, "I need you to set the table while I finish the rolls. Use the wedding china."

Tammy set down her bag and followed her mother into the kitchen. "This is just a casual dinner," she said. "You don't need to use the wedding china." The service for twelve had been a wedding gift from Tammy's great-grandmother, and was only used on holidays and special occasions. The rest of the time, it was displayed in a large buffet on one side of the dining room, dutifully removed and hand-washed each quarter to prevent a buildup of dust.

"This is the first time Mitchell has brought anyone home for dinner." Her mother began shaping dough into rolls and arranging them in a buttered pan. "I want everything to be special."

"You don't have to worry about impressing her, Mom," Tammy said. "She should be worried about impressing you."

"Just looking at Elisabeth, you can tell she comes from money." Mom plopped another roll in the pan. "She's used to fancy things."

"Did Mitch tell you that—that she comes from money?"

She paused in the act of shaping another roll. "No, but it's obvious. Those clothes she wears didn't come from the discount store, and I'm sure her haircut cost at least a hundred dollars."

"If Elisabeth likes Mitch, it's not because he has money," Tammy said, trying to quell her annoyance. "It shouldn't matter what kind of plates we serve dinner on."

"Still, I want to make a good impression."

Tammy went to the buffet and began removing four plates. "If I'd known this was going to be such a big deal, I would have invited a friend," she called back to her mother.

"You can invite your friend some other time," her mother said. "Today, I think the focus should be on Mitch and Elisabeth."

The excitement in her mother's voice set off alarm bells. Tammy returned to the kitchen. "What's going on?" she asked. "Is something happening I should know about?"

Her mother smiled—something she did so seldom the transformation of her features shocked Tammy. "I don't know for sure, but Mitch hinted around that he's serious about this young woman. I think he might propose soon. She could be part of our family before long, and I want her to feel welcomed."

"He's only known her a couple of weeks," Tammy said. "She hasn't even said if she's going to stay in town."

"If they marry, of course she'll stay in Eagle Mountain," her mother said.

Tammy returned to the dining room and tried to process this turn of events as she set the table. Her mother could be wrong. She might be reading more into the relationship than was there.

Then again, Elisabeth's eagerness to have lunch with Tammy last week could have been a way of reaching out to someone she saw as a future sister-in-law. A shudder went through her at the thought; then she immediately felt terrible. If her brother loved Elisabeth, Tammy would learn to love her too.

By the time Mitch and Elisabeth arrived, the table was set with the wedding china and fresh flowers, and the aromas of the Sunday roast and fresh-baked rolls perfumed the air. Elisabeth wore a sleeveless summer sheath in cherry-pink linen, with matching high-heeled sandals. Tammy, dressed in jeans and a T-shirt advertising a defunct local band, reminded herself she had nothing to be defensive about. "It's good to see you," she said.

"Everything looks lovely, Mrs. Patterson," Elisabeth said.

"Not as lovely as you, dear," Mrs. Patterson said. She had changed into slacks and a gauzy top Tammy had never seen before.

"Elisabeth always looks great," Mitch said, and pulled her closer. She smiled up at him, a pleased-with-herself look. Though maybe that was Tammy projecting. She was beginning to realize this wasn't going to be their usual laid-back Sunday meal.

For the next hour, Tammy's mother and brother remained focused on Elisabeth, showering her with compliments and asking her about herself. But while she revealed the same details Tammy already knew—she was from Nebraska and her family had all died—that was all they got. "What kind of work do you do?" Mrs. Patterson asked.

"Oh, I've done a lot of different things," Elisabeth said. "I helped my father manage his investments."

"Do you mean, trading stocks and bonds?" Tammy asked. "Or real estate?"

"Something like that." Elisabeth turned to Mitch. "Mitch had an exciting week. He thinks he's found a buyer for a big ranch near Delta."

Mitch looked pleased. "The deal isn't final yet," he said. "But it's looking promising."

"It would be the largest commission you're earned yet, wouldn't it?" Elisabeth said.

"Yes, it would."

"I could steer you toward some sound investments, if you're interested," Elisabeth said.

Was she legit, or was this some kind of scam? Tammy wondered, then immediately hated herself for thinking it. Her brother was smart enough to see through a scam, even through the rosy lenses of infatuation. And Elisabeth was allowed to be beautiful, charming and good with money.

"What about you, Tammy?" Elisabeth asked. "Did you report on anything particularly interesting this week?"

"The county commissioners agreed to buy a new grader for the road crew," Tammy said. "And the Elks Club has sold almost all of the tickets for the Fourth of July Jeep raffle."

Even Elisabeth's laugh sounded delicate and feminine. "You have to love what passes for news in a small town, don't you?"

"It's reassuring to know there's very little serious crime around here," Mitch said.

"I suppose so," Elisabeth demurred. "Though personally, I never minded a little more excitement."

"Then we'll have to make our own excitement," Mitch said.

Elisabeth smiled at him. "That's an excellent idea."

When the meal ended, Tammy offered to do the dishes.

Better to work off her bad attitude scraping plates than risk taking her annoyance out on her brother's girlfriend.

She was loading the dishwasher when Elisabeth came into the kitchen, a stack of dessert plates in hand. "These were overlooked on the side board," she said, and set them in the sink.

"Thanks," Tammy said.

"Let me help," Elisabeth said.

"No. Go back in with Mitch and Mom. I wouldn't want you to risk getting that beautiful dress dirty."

But Elisabeth made no move to leave. "How's it going with your friend—Vince?" she asked.

Tammy cursed her inability to hold back a blush. "It's going well."

"Did you do what I suggested? Turn up the heat a little?"

Tammy nodded.

"Didn't I tell you?" Elisabeth grinned, and Tammy couldn't help but grin back.

"What are you two plotting in here?" Mitch came in. He stood between them, one arm around each of them. "It's good to see my two favorite women getting along."

"Don't let Mom hear that," Tammy said. "She might feel snubbed."

"My two favorite young women, then." He released his hold on Tammy but took Elisabeth's hand. "Did Elisabeth tell you she's decided to stay in Eagle Mountain?"

"No. That's good news?"

"Of course it's good news," Mitch said. He turned to Elisabeth. "You were asking about my childhood. Mom pulled out her photo albums. You're going to get a laugh out of some of these shots."

They left, still holding hands, and Tammy returned her attention to the dishes. Whatever it was about Elisabeth that

set her teeth on edge, she needed to let it go. She was a pleasant woman who had gone out of her way just now to be
friendly. Tammy would return the favor. She wanted Mitch
to be happy, and if Elisabeth was the one who made him
happy, Tammy needed to find a way to tolerate her, even if
she doubted she could truly love her.

Chapter Fourteen

Once every couple of months, Vince's dad invited Vince to play golf. He didn't have his father's love for the game, but he enjoyed the time they spent, just the two of them, walking the course and talking. Most of the conversations were superficial, but he still relished these moments with the man he admired most in the world.

"When do you think you'll get your truck back?" Dad asked after they had teed off that Sunday afternoon.

"I don't know. The sheriff's department hasn't completed its investigation." He hooked the shot, and the ball went sailing into the rough. "Do you and Mom need your car back? I could borrow one from a friend."

"No, you keep it as long as you like." They trudged toward Vince's wayward ball. "I was just wondering. Do they have any idea who did it?"

Vince lined up his shot and took it, hitting the ball back onto the fairway. "No. The sheriff asked if I thought it could be Valerie."

He expected his dad to be shocked or to protest that that wasn't possible. Instead, he looked thoughtful. "I've often wondered if she is still alive somewhere."

"Why do you think that?"

"Take your shot, son."

Vince's heart wasn't in the next strokes, but he managed to keep the ball on the fairway and eventually in the hole.

His dad led the way to the next tee box. "Why do you think Valerie is still alive?" Vince asked again. Had his dad been keeping something secret from him all this time?

"I suppose because we never found her," he said. "And because she's my daughter. It's a fanciful idea, I guess, but if she's dead, wouldn't I feel it? I know your mother feels the same way."

What did Vince feel? Valerie was his twin, yet he had long ago accepted she was dead. But what if she wasn't?

He waited until his dad had taken his shot before he spoke again. "If Valerie is alive, why not contact us?" he asked. "Why write cryptic notes or mess up my truck?"

"Maybe she's under someone else's control and this is her only way to communicate." He swung and connected with the ball, sending it straight up the fairway. He was so calm that Vince realized he must have spent a lot of time thinking about this possibility.

"Dad, she'd be twenty-five years old now. How could she be under someone else's control?"

"Someone could be threatening her, forcing her to do these things."

"But why? No one has asked for money. No one has tried to physically harm us. It's just…annoying." He took his stroke and sliced the ball to the right.

"And a little frightening." Dad put his hand on Vince's shoulder, a rare moment of physical closeness from his normally undemonstrative father.

"Yeah, it is frightening," Vince admitted. "I keep wondering what's going to happen next."

"If they want something, you'll find out," his dad said.

"Scammers are experts at the long game, reeling people in slowly."

"Is that what happened with you and that guy who claimed to be ex–special forces? The one you and Mom paid all that money to?" That had been a particularly elaborate scam, and a costly one. The man claimed Valerie was being held prisoner in a Mexican brothel, and that, with funds for their expenses, he and some other former military friends could rescue her.

His dad looked rueful. "I thought I was smart enough to see through all the liars by that time. Valerie had been missing five years, and I thought I had heard it all. But this man was a pro. He presented just the right image. I resisted him for a long time, but then he sent pictures—photographs of a young woman he claimed was Valerie. We could only see her from the back—that should have been my first clue this wasn't legit. But she had the same hair, and we could see the resemblance. He said if we paid for him and a team to fly down there, they promised to get her back. We wanted so much to believe, and he counted on that."

Vince's chest hurt, listening to this sad tale, even though he had known the basic outline for a long time. "I think anyone would have done the same in your shoes," he said.

They played through the next hole, the heaviness of their memories wrapped around them. After Vince's next shot, his dad said, "I never told your mother this, but I thought I saw Valerie once."

Vince's breath caught, and he stared. "Where? When?"

"Seven years ago. I had a work meeting outside of Omaha, Nebraska. A group of us visited a casino on the Missouri river one evening. There was this cocktail waitress—pretty, young, very friendly. I noticed her, but I wasn't paying any particular attention to her. Then one of the guys nudged me and told me she obviously liked me because she kept staring at me. I looked over, and she caught my eye and smiled. And—I recognized her. It was Valerie."

"In a casino in Omaha? Dad, why did you think it was Valerie?"

"Her eyes, and the way she looked at me. I hurried toward her, but she darted away. I spent the rest of the night searching for her. I even went back the following day and asked the manager about her. He said they didn't have any employees that fit the description I gave them. But I know what I saw."

"What did you do?" Vince asked.

"I took an extra day after the conference. I went back to the casino, then spent hours driving around the area. I guess I thought I might spot her again, but if she didn't want to be seen, there were a million places she could hide. I finally convinced myself that I must have been mistaken. I went back home and tried to forget about her. But I've always wondered."

"If Valerie is alive, I have to think she would want to see us," Vince said. "We're her family."

"I like to think that too, son. But we don't know what she's been through in the time she's been apart from us."

She isn't alive, he wanted to say but didn't. If it made his father feel better to believe his daughter wasn't dead, Vince wasn't going to dissuade him. But that kind of hope felt to Vince like a chain holding them all back. Valerie was dead. Until they accepted that, they could never move on.

MONDAY, TAMMY TRIED to focus on work, but her mind continually drifted to thoughts of Vince, replaying the two amazing evenings they had spent together. She thought she had been head over heels for a man before. The giddy sensation of wanting to be with someone every minute wasn't new.

But things with Vince were different. More intense, yet less stressful. They connected in a way she hadn't known was possible, and didn't feel any pressure to hide the "weird" side of herself from him. She hadn't realized how much she was holding back in other relationships until she got close to Vince.

"What are you grinning about?" Russ asked as he passed her desk that afternoon.

She immediately assumed a sober expression. "Nothing," she said.

"What are you working on?" he asked.

She glanced at her computer screen, the cursor blinking on the beginning of an unwritten paragraph—the same position it had been in for the last half hour. She started to repeat *Nothing* but thought better of it. "I'm writing that piece about the women's club rummage sale," she said. "And I'm finishing up my next piece about search and rescue."

"Don't forget the planning commission meeting at six."

She groaned. "Nothing ever happens at those meetings."

"Then why are they having a meeting?" he asked.

"So they can table making a decision on land-use codes— the same thing they've done the last three meetings."

"They can't table a decision forever," Russ said. "And when they reach a conclusion, our readers will want to know what it is."

She sighed. Russ was right, of course. And she did have the meeting on her calendar. It was just that she would 100 percent have preferred to spend the evening with Vince.

But the meeting did give her an excuse to text him. Though they hadn't made definite plans for tonight, she sensed that spending every night together was becoming a habit neither was in a hurry to break.

Can't get together tonight, she typed. I've got to cover the planning commission meeting.

She pressed Send and waited, not exactly holding her breath but unable to look away from the screen.

The phone vibrated, and a small thrill raced through her as she read his reply. Too bad. Guess I'll have to sit at home alone and think about my plans for next time we get together.

She started to type a reply asking for more specifics about what he had in mind but became aware of Russ watching her. "You're grinning again," he said.

She frowned and turned the phone so the screen was definitely out of Russ's line of sight. Looking forward to seeing you again, she typed. TTYL.

The meeting that evening proved as boring as she had anticipated, though the commission did spring for pizza from Mo's to feed themselves, Tammy and the two locals who showed up. At least she didn't have to listen to them debate the exact definition of *agricultural use* on an empty stomach.

By nine o'clock everyone in the room seemed to have had enough. The committee had agreed on some definitions and tabled other decisions until the following month. Tammy gathered her belongings and drove home. She debated dropping by to see Vince but decided instead to call him when she got in.

Her mind played out possible avenues for such a conversation as she climbed out of her car and headed up the walkway to her house.

Then something—or rather, someone—hit her with such force she was knocked off her feet. She didn't even have time to scream before her attacker landed on top of her and began pummeling her.

Chapter Fifteen

For a moment Tammy couldn't fight back or even breathe. She forced her eyes open, trying to see who was hitting her, but could make out only the shadowy outline of a figure dressed in dark clothing. Her attacker grabbed her hair and forced her head back, then rammed it into the dirt.

Pain rocketed through her and freed her from her momentary paralysis. She shoved against her assailant, then brought her knee up, hard, between the other person's legs. The reaction wasn't the one she had expected. Her attacker grunted, then laughed.

Whoever this was, Tammy realized they weren't much bigger than her. Another shove pushed them off her. She kicked out again, this time connecting with the other person's shin. She grabbed for any hold she could find and wrapped her hand around an ear and pulled hard.

This time her attacker screamed—a high-pitched wail of rage. They staggered up and began kicking at Tammy, who rolled away, then shoved to her knees.

By the time she got to her feet, whoever had assaulted her was running away, feet pounding hard on the pavement. Tammy stood, staggering a little as a wave of dizziness rocked her. The front door creaked open. "Tammy? Is that you?" her mother's voice asked.

The words forced her into action. She hurried to the door and gently urged her mother back inside. "Let's go in, Mom." She followed her mom into the front hall and locked the door behind them.

Mrs. Patterson stared at her daughter. "You're bleeding!" she said. "What happened?"

Tammy turned to the mirror by the door. Blood trickled from her swollen lip, and her hair was sticky with clotting blood. One eye was starting to swell, and her shirt was torn. "Someone attacked me right in our driveway," she said.

"We need to call the sheriff." Her mother looked around, as if searching for a phone.

"Yes. You'd better do that."

While her mother dialed 911 and talked to the operator, Tammy went to one of the front windows and peered out. Hers was the only vehicle visible near the house, and she could see no sign of her attacker, though the darkness past the circle of light from the porch was so intense she could scarcely make out anything.

"They're sending a deputy right away." Her mother came to stand beside her. "Let me clean up that cut," she said.

"No, thanks. I'll be okay until after the deputy gets here. They may want to take pictures or something." Was that only in cases of rape? Had that been the attacker's intent? This felt like violence for the sake of violence. Someone wanted to hurt her.

Deputy Declan Owen knocked on the door approximately ten minutes later. The handsome dark-haired deputy was relatively new to the Rayford County Sheriff's Department, but he had impressed Tammy as smart and professional. He studied her battered face for a moment when she opened the door, then said, "Why don't we sit down somewhere, and you can tell me what happened."

She led him to the living room, where they sat on either end of the sofa. Her mother took the armchair nearest Tammy and perched on the edge of the seat, hands knotted together. "I drove home from the planning-commission meeting, parked my car and started up the walkway," Tammy said. "Then someone attacked me. I hit the ground hard, my attacker on top of me, pummeling me. We wrestled for a few minutes, then I managed to fight them off and they ran away."

"Did you see your attacker?" Declan asked. "Can you describe them?"

She shook her head. "It was dark, and I think they were wearing dark clothing. I think they even had something covering their face, like a balaclava."

"How big a person? Did they say anything? Could you tell if it was a man or a woman?"

"Not much bigger than me," she said. "I think that's why I was able to shove them off. And I think… I don't think it was a man. They felt—softer. Like a woman. And…and I kicked them hard between the legs, and while they didn't like it, it didn't exactly disable them."

Declan made more notes on the pad in his hand. "Did they say anything?"

"Not a word."

"Do you have any idea who this was?"

"No. I don't know why anyone would attack me. Especially another woman."

"Anyone who might be upset by an article you've written lately?"

"No. I haven't written anything controversial lately. And when people get upset by an article, they write angry letters to the editor. Or they tell me to my face what I did wrong. This person just started hitting me without saying anything."

"Could it be a jealous girlfriend or wife who thinks you're involved with their husband or boyfriend?"

"No. I haven't been dating anyone." She blushed. "Well, I'm sort of seeing Vince Shepherd. But he doesn't have a girlfriend, or a wife." Not that she knew of, anyway.

Declan turned to Tammy's mom. "Did you see anything unusual this evening before Tammy came home?" he asked. "A strange car in the neighborhood, maybe someone who stopped by the house, looking for her?"

"No. I didn't know anything was going on until I heard a scream. I went to the door to see if Tammy had fallen in the dark or something."

"Did you get a glimpse of her attacker?" Declan asked.

"I'm sorry, no." Her mother frowned at Tammy. "I didn't know you were dating anyone."

"Vince and I are taking things slow," she said. She turned to Declan. "Have there been any other attacks like this?"

"No," Declan said. "Is there anything else you can tell us about the person who attacked you? Did they have long or short hair, or anything that stood out to you?"

"I think they had their hair covered, perhaps by the balaclava. I didn't feel any hair. Whoever it was, they were strong—and angry." She touched her swollen lip. "I need to clean up and get some ice on my face."

Declan stood. "I'll talk to your neighbors and see if any of them noticed anyone hanging around who shouldn't be in the area. Let us know if you think of anything else."

Tammy walked with him to the door. As soon as he was gone, her mother started fussing. "We should go to the hospital," she said. "You might need stitches."

"I'll be okay, Mom. I'm going to take a shower, then go to bed." The fight had left her exhausted, and in no mood to talk to anyone. Not even Vince.

"I'm going to call Mitch and ask him to come over."

"Mom, no. He's probably with Elisabeth."

"I don't care. I'll feel a lot safer with him here. She can come with him, if she likes."

Tammy studied her mother's placid expression. "You like her, don't you?"

"I like that she makes your brother happy. That's what I want most for both of you children."

"Do you worry that she's not right for him?"

"The most unlikely couples can make a good match," her mother said. "As long as each partner has an equal stake in making things work. Otherwise, there's going to be trouble ahead."

Tammy retreated to her bathroom. If she let herself, those terrifying moments on the ground with her assailant would replay themselves over and over and in her mind. Instead, she thought about Vince. The two of them seemed equally matched. And they were both equally hesitant to be hurt. Did that bode well for their future or mean they were condemned to never get close enough to last?

THE SEARCH AND rescue training Tuesday evening was mandatory for rookies like Vince, who were preparing for their SARTech II certification test. He took a seat at the end of a table, next to Grace Wilcox. Bethany turned to smile at him. "Hi, Vince," she said.

"Hey." The intensity with which she studied him unnerved him. He didn't want to be unfriendly, but he didn't want to encourage her attention either.

"Don't you have anything better to do on a Tuesday night?" Grace Wilcox asked as Eldon slipped past them to settle on her other side.

"It never hurts to refresh my memory," Eldon said. He

picked up a pencil and slotted it behind one ear. "Plus, May is out of town at an art show, and there's nothing good on TV. I might as well be here."

Danny moved to the front of the room. "Let's get started, everyone. Somebody dim the lights." He hit the button for the first slide. "We're going to start with some definitions."

A loud creak from the door interrupted him. Everyone in the room turned to see Tammy slip inside. "Sorry I'm late," she said, and took a seat at the back of the room. She had her head down, hair falling over one eye. Vince sat up straighter and tried to get a better look. Normally, he expected her to smile and maybe search the room for him, but she wasn't doing that. Was something wrong?

"It's okay," Danny said. "Let's get started with the first section."

They took a break after the first hour, and Vince made his way toward Tammy. He stopped short when she turned to look at him. One eye was swollen shut, and her lips were puffy. "What happened to you?" he asked. At the sound of his voice, everyone who hadn't already been looking their way turned toward them.

Tammy's face reddened. "Somebody jumped me outside my house last night when I got home from the meeting," she said. She put a hand on his arm. "I'm okay. Really."

"Who was it?" Eldon asked.

"I don't know," she said. "It was dark and I didn't see a lot, and they never said anything. I fought them off, and they ran away. Apparently, none of the neighbors saw anyone suspicious in the area." She put a hand to her face. "I know I look terrible."

"You look fine." Vince hesitated, then put an arm around her. "But I hate that you were hurt." He leaned closer and spoke more softly into her ear. "Why didn't you tell me?"

"I didn't want to upset you," she said. "You've got enough on your mind right now."

"Not too much to care about what happens to you," he said.

This made her smile, though she immediately winced, probably because her lip hurt.

"Are you thinking of joining search and rescue?" Bethany asked. She had moved up on Vince's other side and was studying Tammy with that piercing way of hers.

Tammy looked grateful for the change of subject. "No. I told Danny I wanted to write more about the training you guys undergo, and he suggested I attend the class tonight."

"It's an overview of the general knowledge we need to have," Danny said. "Though there's a lot more that goes into wilderness rescues."

"So I'm learning," she said.

"Is that your next article, about training?" Caleb asked.

"No. I'm going to write about the Denise Darling case."

A buzz arose as several people asked about Denise Darling, and others rushed to explain. Danny, being the most senior volunteer present, gained the floor. "She was a thirteen-year-old girl who disappeared during a youth hiking trip seven years ago," he said. "She became separated from her group and got lost. She was found eight days later, almost ten miles from the place she had last been seen."

"Was she alive?" Bethany asked.

"She was alive." Vince hadn't realized he had spoken loudly enough to be heard until everyone turned to him. "I remember the story," he added. "It was all anyone talked about for a while." And he remembered it because of Valerie. When Denise Darling had been found, his mother had burst into sobs. Not because she wasn't glad that a girl had been restored to her family, but because the same thing had never happened to them. Why wasn't Valerie ever found?

"I wonder what became of her," Danny said. "She did an amazing job of taking care of herself—better than most adults under similar circumstances."

"I'm still trying to locate her for an interview," Tammy said. "If I do, I'll let you know."

Danny checked his watch. "We'd better get back to work, or we'll be here all night."

Vince tried to focus on the material, but he kept looking back at Tammy's battered face. Who would hurt her that way?

He hoped the notes he was taking would help him cram for the SARTech test, because he had been too distracted to absorb much information tonight. As soon as Danny turned the lights up, he was out of his chair and headed for Tammy. She smiled at his approach. "Don't look so worried," she said. "I really am all right."

"Where did this happen?" he asked.

"Right in front of my house. I think the person might have been waiting for me. Either that or they followed me home from the planning-commission meeting."

"You're not making me less worried," he said.

She took both his hands in hers and squeezed. "Mitch is staying at the house for a while," she said. "I guess it does feel safer having him there."

"You're welcome to stay with me whenever you like."

"I like that idea." She rose on tiptoe and pressed her lips to his. He wrapped his arms around her and turned it into a proper kiss.

A shrill whistle sounded. "Hey, get a room!" someone shouted, followed by raucous laughter.

They pulled apart. "Why don't I follow you home?" she

said, and reached for her car door. She immediately recoiled, and let out a moan.

"What is it?" Vince took her arm. "What's wrong?"

She pointed, and now he saw that something red was smeared across the car door and windshield. He leaned around to examine the windshield and went cold all over when he read the message scrawled in the same red across the glass: *Next time you won't be so lucky. V.*

Chapter Sixteen

"It's not blood." Paramedic Hannah Gwynn cleaned the red goo from Tammy's hand. A crowd had gathered around the Subaru, and someone said the sheriff's department was on the way. Another volunteer had switched on the outdoor spotlights on the side of the building, flooding the gravel parking area with yellow-tinged light.

"I think it's stage blood." Jake Gwynn leaned closer to the car to study the smears of red. "It smells sweet, like corn syrup."

"Why would someone leave you a message like that?" Eldon asked.

"It's because of me," Vince said. His face was pale, the muscles along his jaw tight, as if he was grinding his teeth. He had both hands shoved in the pockets of his jeans and kept sneaking looks at Tammy, though he wouldn't directly meet her gaze.

Her hands clean, she moved to his side and took his arm. "This isn't your fault," she said.

"This was done by the same person who trashed my truck," he said. "It's probably the same person who attacked you last night."

"You can't know that," she said.

"The signature is the same." He pointed to the message on the side window.

She read the threatening words again, freezing when she came to the single *V*, like a check mark near the driver's-side windshield wiper. "I didn't notice the V before," she said.

"The message does seem to be referring to your previous assault," Jake said. "And I'm no expert on graffiti, but this looks similar to the writing on Vince's truck."

"At least they didn't smash my windows." She was trying to make a joke, but the effect was spoiled when her voice broke on the final words.

The crunch of tires on gravel signaled the arrival of a sheriff's department SUV. Sergeant Gage Walker exited the vehicle and strode toward them. Tammy had interviewed Gage many times for cases she had reported. Though similar in appearance to his brother, the sheriff, Gage was more easygoing and less intimidating. He nodded to Tammy, then studied the red-smeared car and the sinister message. Then he turned to the crowd. "I'll talk to the rest of you in a bit. Meanwhile, give us some room, will you?"

The others moved away, herded by Jake. Gage turned back to Tammy. "Tough way to end the night," he said.

"It sure is."

"Any ideas who's behind this and the attack on you last night?" he asked.

"None."

"I think it's the same person who trashed my truck," Vince said. "The same person who sent those notes about Valerie."

"*V*," Gage said. He stepped back and took a few photos of the car, then turned to Tammy. "Why threaten you?" he asked.

She glanced at Vince. Their relationship wasn't exactly a secret, but she also wasn't sure where they stood. "Tammy and I are friends," he said. "Good friends. If this 'V' has been watching me, they've seen us together. Maybe they think hurting Tammy is a way to get back at me."

"I read the report on your assault," Gage said. "You told Declan you thought your assailant was a woman?"

"Yes." Vince frowned at her. Something else she hadn't told him. But again, she hadn't wanted him to worry. If V and her attacker were the same person, did that mean it was Valerie? Or someone pretending to be her?

"Why would V want to get back at you?" Gage asked.

"I'm not sure whoever this is has a reason," she said. "Or at least, not one that would make sense to us."

"In some of the communications, V seems to be assuming the role of Valerie," Vince said.

"Any chance this is your sister?" Gage asked.

"The sheriff asked me that too," Vince said. "I don't know. Valerie disappeared fifteen years ago. Why appear out of nowhere now, and why try to hurt me?"

"When you came here tonight, did you see anyone or anything out of the ordinary?" Gage asked.

"No. And I was looking. After what happened last night, I was spooked."

Gage took her through her steps that evening, from the time she left the newspaper office until she drove to search and rescue headquarters, and verified that she was the last person to arrive at the meeting.

"No one arrived or left after you?" Gage asked.

"No one," she said.

"I didn't see anyone come or go," Vince said.

"All right. We'll process the scene and see if we come up with anything," Gage said. "You'll need to leave your car here. Do you have someplace safe to stay tonight? And what about your mother? Is she home alone?"

"My brother is with her. He's moved in temporarily."

"I'll see that Tammy gets somewhere safe," Vince said. He straightened and took his hands from his pockets. "Do you need anything else?"

"Not right now," Gage said. "I may have more questions later."

"I have a backpack in the car I'd like to grab," she said.

Gage slipped on a glove and opened the back door of the vehicle, and waited while she leaned in and took out the backpack. "Check to verify nothing is missing," he said.

She did so, pawing through the notebooks, extra camera battery, tape recorder and other tools of her trade. "Everything looks okay."

"You're free to go, then."

Vince led her a little ways to the white Ford Escape he was driving these days. "It's my mother's," he said by way of explanation.

Tammy stashed her pack in the back seat, then slid into the passenger seat. Vince drove without speaking, not to her home but to his condo. "I'd feel better if you stayed here tonight," he said. "You can call your mother and brother to let them know you're okay."

"I'd like that." Spending the night alone, even with her brother and mother in other parts of the house, would be too uncomfortable. Even though Vince might be right and the attacks on her might be because V was targeting him, she felt safer with him beside her. If V came around again, it would be two against one.

He carried her pack into the house. Once inside, he pulled her close. "I felt awful when I saw you tonight, hurt." He brushed his lips across her swollen eye, then barely touched her wounded lip. "When I think I could have lost you—" His voice broke.

"You didn't lose me. I'm okay and I'm right here." She

kissed him. It didn't hurt. Instead it felt good, the way his strong arms around her felt good. The kiss ended, and she looked into his eyes, trying to judge what he was feeling. "I'm sorry I didn't tell you about the attack right away. It was just…a lot to process. I wanted time to think."

"You think it was a woman?" he asked.

"I think so. She wasn't much bigger than me, and she didn't feel like a man."

He loosened his hold on her a little. "What do you want to do now?" he asked.

"I can think of a few things." She smiled. "But first, I want to take a shower." Her hand was still slightly sticky from the fake blood, and she wanted to wash away the whole experience.

"Let's take one together," he said.

"Mmm." A pleasant heat washed through her at the thought. "Let me call my mom first so she doesn't worry."

She was surprised when her brother answered the phone. "Mitch, why are you answering Mom's phone?"

"She's in the bathroom and I saw the call was from you. What's up?"

Maybe it was better not to have to explain everything to her mother. "I'm staying with a friend tonight," she said.

"Do you mean, Vince Shepherd?"

"How do you know about Vince?"

"Elisabeth told me you and he had something going on. I'm cool with that, as long as he treats you right."

"I don't need your permission to date someone," she said.

"I'm just saying I think Vince is okay. Don't be so touchy."

"Is Elisabeth there with you?"

"No. She said she had something else to do tonight. To tell you the truth, I think she was uncomfortable with the idea of being here with you and Mom. She thinks the two of you don't like her."

"That's not true," Tammy said. "We hardly know her."

"Yeah, well, it's okay. I'll see her tomorrow."

"And I'll see you tomorrow," she said. "Make sure Mom knows I'm okay."

"Have a good night."

She ended the call and pocketed her phone. "Everything okay?" Vince asked.

"It's fine." She moved closer. She didn't want to talk about her brother or Elisabeth or anything outside the safety of these four walls. She wrapped her arms around him. "What about that shower?"

VINCE LAY AWAKE after Tammy had fallen asleep. He might never think about his shower the same way after tonight. Something about steam and soap and slick skin… It had been just what he needed after the shock of seeing her battered face, then reading the sinister message written in what he was sure was supposed to resemble blood on her car.

His phone vibrated, then the first notes of the ringtone sounded. He lunged for it, silencing it before it could wake Tammy. Then he sat on the side of the bed and checked the screen as the phone continued to vibrate in his hand. Unknown number. Which usually meant spam, but he'd better check in case it was a search and rescue call from one of the team members.

He spoke softly. "Hello?"

"Vin, Vin, Vinnie, Vince."

The singsong chant sent a cold shock through him. "Who is this?" he snapped.

"'Vince and Tammy sitting in a tree, *k-i-s-s-i-n-g*.'"

"Who is this?"

"You know who this is. Or have you forgotten your sister so soon? The twin Mommy and Daddy gave away. You thought you would all be happier without me. But I can't let that happen, can I?"

"Valerie?" He choked on the name as fear and disgust— that someone would stoop to impersonating his sister— warred with hope that she was alive. "Is that you? Where are you?"

"Closer than you think. But I'll never tell."

"Valerie, I—" The phone went dead. He stared at the screen, then hit the recall button. Nothing happened.

"What is it?"

He glanced back to find that Tammy had rolled onto her back and was looking at him. "Crank call," he said, and set the phone aside.

"You said, 'Valerie.'" She sat up now and put a hand on his arm. "Tell me."

He told her about the call. The whole experience had been surreal, but talking about it solidified the details in his mind. He hadn't dreamed it. "Did it sound like Valerie?" she asked.

"I don't remember what she sounds like. It was so long ago. But she used to sing that rhyme, about kissing in a tree."

"I used to sing that rhyme. It's something kids do."

"She started out the call saying 'Vin, Vin, Vinnie, Vincent.' She used to do that too, when she was trying to annoy me."

She leaned against him, soft and warm against his back. "We should call the sheriff."

"What are they going to do? Add this to their growing file of harassment?" He lay back down and pulled her close. "I don't want to deal with them now. Do you?"

"No." She laid her head on his shoulder.

"I had another call from Valerie once," he said. "Or someone claiming to be her. I was fifteen and home with a friend. My parents were out, and when I answered the phone, the person on the other end said she was Valerie and needed me to help her. Then she hung up. It sounded just like her."

"Oh, Vince, what did you do?"

"I told my parents and they called the police. They traced the call to a broken pay phone somewhere in another state. I remember being angry at Valerie for teasing me that way. My parents finally persuaded me that it had to be a cruel joke. This was probably the same thing."

"Whatever it is, it's horrible," she said. "But we'll get through it. Together."

"Yeah." He tightened his arm around her. As if that was all it took to protect them both. "I'm scared," he said. "Then it feels silly to be scared of someone who writes vague notes and makes prank calls."

"It's like being harassed by a ghost," she said. "That's pretty scary."

"I don't believe in ghosts," he said. "Whoever is doing this is a real person."

"I don't know what to tell you, except that I'm here for you."

"As long as you don't get hurt again. You should think about keeping your distance from me, at least for a while." He had to force the words out, but keeping her safe was more important than his own feelings.

"No way." She squeezed him tighter. "I'm sticking with you."

"I'm that irresistible, am I?"

"You are."

"I'm never going to be able to sleep now," he said.

"Me neither. What should we do instead?"

"We could play cards," he said, his voice teasing.

Her arm snaked around his waist. "I have a better idea."

"Tell me about it."

"I'd rather show you. After all, they say actions speak louder than words."

He rolled forward and pressed his body against hers. "Then I'm ready to hear everything you have to say."

ON WEDNESDAY, Gage Walker stopped by the *Eagle Mountain Examiner* office. Tammy's stomach gave a nervous shimmy when she spotted him standing in the doorway in his neat khaki uniform. "Hello, Gage," she said. "Can I help you?"

"I'm dropping off the weekly sheriff's report." He held up a single sheet of paper. The report—a summary of the number and types of calls made by the department during the previous week—was one of the paper's most popular features. People seemed to delight in reading about calls to chase bears out of people's gardens or put cows back into pastures. They speculated on who might be behind the more serious entries, from drunk driving arrests to domestic violence calls. But the report was usually delivered by a civilian clerk or a duty officer, not the force's second-in-command.

Gage approached Tammy's desk and handed over the report. "Any more word from V?" he asked.

"No. She hasn't contacted me." It seemed easier to refer to V as female since that was how she thought of her since the attack.

"What about Vince? Has he heard anything?"

"I don't think so." She had never been a proficient liar, and she was sure Gage would see through the falsehood. She had tried to persuade Vince to tell the sheriff's department about the late-night call from someone pretending to be Valerie, but he had refused, convinced they wouldn't be able to do anything.

"Did you find any fingerprints or DNA on my car?" she asked, hoping to divert Gage's attention.

"No. Not on Vince's truck either." He held up a finger. "But that's not for the paper."

"I know, Gage. I'm not writing about either incident."

"I just want to be clear. Tell Vince to get in touch if he hears anything else from V."

"I will." She stood and walked with him to the door. "I guess I'll see you at the Fourth of July festivities tomorrow?"

"I'm on duty in the morning," he said. "In the afternoon, I'm working the Elks' Fun Fair."

"I'll stop and say hello. Maybe get a picture for the paper."

When she was sure he was gone, she went into the back room, where old issues of the paper were stored, and pulled out her phone. When Vince answered, she said, "Gage was just here. He was asking if I had heard anything from V."

"What did you tell him?"

"I told him no. That wasn't exactly a lie, since she didn't call me. But then he asked if you had heard from her. I lied about that too."

"It doesn't matter. It was just a prank call. We haven't heard from her again."

"You're working the Fun Fair tomorrow, right? So is Gage. He'll probably ask you about V."

"My parents will be with me. I'll tell him I don't want to talk about any of this with them there. He'll respect that."

"Okay. I'll see you later, then."

"I'm making fajitas for dinner."

"Then I won't be late."

Though it wasn't official, she had all but moved into Vince's condo. Her mother hadn't even objected when she stopped by the house to get her clothes. "I feel better knowing you have a man to protect you," she said.

The feminist in Tammy resented the implication she couldn't look after herself, but the realist admitted having a strong, fit man who had made it clear he would do anything to protect her did make her feel safer. What neither of them admitted out loud was that they wouldn't be able to truly relax until V was identified and stopped. That didn't seem likely to happen anytime soon, so better for the two of them to stick together.

Chapter Seventeen

The next day, Tammy and Vince headed to the town park together. "How are you feeling?" he asked when they met, He studied her face. "The swelling is almost all gone and the bruises aren't as noticeable."

She resisted the urge to touch the worst of the bruises, which she had attempted to cover with makeup. "I'm fine. Really."

"Glad to hear it." He kept his arm around her on the walk to the park, but once there, they parted ways. Tammy was taking photographs of the parade while Vince helped set up the search and rescue booth. Later, she would take pictures of the Fun Fair while he fulfilled his duties at the SAR booth and the first responders' part in the festivities. He was also meeting his parents to spend time with them. The plan was for her to join them as soon as she was free. Later that evening, they would enjoy the fireworks.

The Eagle Mountain Fourth of July Parade was everything a small-town parade should be, from the high school marching band to dignitaries waving from fire trucks to clusters of kids pedaling red, white and blue-bedecked bicycles. Members of the historical society, dressed in turn-of-the-last-century garb, threw candy from a float decorated with papier-mâché rocks and old mining implements, while a trio of miniature horses and one full-size camel from a local hobby ranch enchanted onlookers.

The mayor's six-year-old son brought up the rear of the parade, riding a donkey with a placard attached to its backside that read *Follow My Ass to the First Responders Fun Fair.*

After a detour to photograph the historical society members handing out lemonade and brownies in front of the town museum, Tammy headed for the park, where the Fun Fair was in full swing. At the search and rescue booth, which was festooned with colorful T-shirts for sale and photographs from past rescues, she learned that Vince had just completed his shift. She took a photo to possibly run with her article, then hurried across the park, where she found Gage Walker supervising a pillow fight between two boys who straddled a sawhorse and flailed at each other until one slid to the sawdust below.

"Have you seen Vince?" she asked Gage after he had helped the children to their feet and sent them on their way.

"I think he's over at the dunking booth." Gage grinned. "He's probably pretty wet by now."

She had to stop and ask two people for directions to the dunking booth, but she arrived in time to see Vince, in swim trunks and nothing else, climb onto the narrow perch over a tank of water. "Just remember, that water's really cold," Deputy Shane Ellis teased Vince, egging on the crowd. "Five dollars for three throws," he said, holding up a baseball. "All the money goes to local first responders. Who wants to throw out the first pitch?"

"Why don't you show us how it's done, Shane?" someone called from the crowd.

"That wouldn't be fair, would it?" Shane demurred. He was a former big-league pitcher. Though an injury had ended his career, he was still feared on the local softball field.

"I'll go first." Ryan Welch stepped forward and handed over a five-dollar bill. His first pitch went wild, banging hard against the wood to the left of the target.

"A little more finesse there," Shane advised.

The second throw came closer but still failed to hit the bull's-eye.

"Come on," Vince taunted. "I'm getting hot up here."

Ryan clenched his jaw and palmed the ball, then hurled it, striking the bull's-eye dead center and sending Vince plunging into the tank.

He came up sputtering and laughing as the crowd cheered. Tammy snapped a series of photos; then he returned to his perch and Shane called for someone else to take a turn.

"Hey, Tammy."

She turned to see Mitch and Elisabeth working their way to her through the crowd. "So, that's Vince!" Elisabeth waggled her eyebrows at Tammy.

Mitch looked toward the dunk tank. "Looks like he's all wet," he said.

"Even better, huh?" She nudged Tammy.

"Anyone else want to take a try?" Shane called.

"I'll do it." Mitch raised his hand and pushed forward.

Elisabeth moved in closer to Tammy. "I didn't know Mitch was an athlete," she said.

"He's not." Tammy winced as her brother's first ball sailed past the dunk tank altogether. A trio of children chased after it.

"Steady there, Rocket," Shane said, and handed him another ball. "Go a little easier."

Mitch nodded and launched the second ball, which bounced harmlessly off the side of the tank.

Elisabeth cupped her hands around her mouth. "Go, Mitch!" she shouted.

Mitch waved back at her, then turned and fired the third ball toward the target. It glanced off the edge, but without enough force to trip the trigger. The crowd groaned.

"Let me have a try!" Elisabeth called, and waved her hand.

Applause greeted her arrival. To the delight of the crowd, she dusted off the ball with her shirt, then leaned forward like a pitcher waiting for a sign. Then she straightened and let the ball fly. It landed harmlessly in the grass, just shy of the target.

"Put a little more behind it this time," Shane advised, and handed her a second ball.

This one struck to the left of the target. Vince clapped his hands together. "You can do better than that!" he shouted.

Elisabeth glared at him and accepted the third ball. This time she stared not at the target, but at Vince, until he looked away. She wound up, then let the ball fly. It hit the center of the target, and Vince went down with a shout. The crowd roared its approval.

"Way to go, babe," Mitch said as Elisabeth rejoined him. He hugged her close. She accepted congratulations from those around her.

"That was fun," she said. "What should we do now?"

"I don't know," Mitch said. "Do you want—"

But before he could finish the sentence, Elisabeth was moving away. "I just saw someone I need to talk to," she called over her shoulder, and was gone.

"What was that about?" Tammy asked.

"I don't know." Mitch stared after her. She was weaving through the crowd, already a quarter of the way across the park. "I'd better go after her," he said, and left.

"It's Tammy, isn't it?" An older couple squeezed in beside her. The woman smiled. "I'm Vince's mom. I thought I recognized you from your picture in the paper."

"It's good to meet you." She nodded to Mr. Shepherd.

"Have you been here long?" Mrs. Shepherd asked.

"Long enough to see Vince get dunked twice," Tammy said.

"Us too." Mr. Shepherd smiled, fine lines deepening at the corners of his eyes. "He looks like he's having fun up there."

A loud creak and a cheer from the crowd signaled that Vince had once again been dunked. "Three strikes and you're out," Shane announced. "Give us a few minutes, folks, and we'll have your next victim—I mean, volunteer—up."

He handed Vince a towel as he emerged from the tank. "Let's go see if he's ready for lunch," Mrs. Shepherd said.

The three of them met Vince as he was pulling on a T-shirt. "Give me a second to change into dry pants, and we'll get some food," he said.

"It's good to see you," Mrs. Shepherd said to Tammy. "Are you working on anything interesting right now?"

"I'm doing another piece about the search and rescue team," she said.

"Vince has told us about some of the rescues he's been on," Mrs. Shepherd said. "We're so proud of him for volunteering, though I worry about the dangerous situations he gets into."

"One thing I've learned in researching my articles is that the search and rescue team trains a lot, and they always put safety first. They've never lost a rescuer."

"That's reassuring."

Vince joined them. He put one arm around Tammy. "Can you join us for lunch?" he asked. "Or do you have to work?"

"I might try to get a few shots of the fireworks tonight, but I'm free for the rest of the afternoon."

"Great. Let's hit the food booths. I'm starved."

They followed the scent of barbecue ribs and roasted corn to a parking lot filled with food trucks and refreshment booths. Tammy ordered shrimp tempura from one truck, while Vince and his dad opted for the ribs, and Mrs. Shepherd chose a hot dog. "That looks delicious," she said, nodding to Tammy's tempura. "But I guess I'm a traditionalist."

"We always grilled hot dogs and brats on the Fourth when the kids were little," Mr. Shepherd said.

Someone who wasn't watching closely would have missed the sadness that fleetingly shadowed Vince's mother's face. Though she had acted cheerful all morning, now that she was closer, Tammy could read the strain in the dark circles beneath her eyes and the slight tremor in her hand as she poked a straw into her drink. When she noticed Tammy watching her, she leaned closer. "You haven't heard anything more from V, have you?" she asked softly.

"No." Vince had told her he had decided not to tell his parents about the attack on her, the message on her car or the late-night phone call. "Hearing all that would just upset and worry them," he had said. She had agreed. As much as she hated the harassment V had aimed at her and Vince, at least she hadn't targeted these two older people, who had suffered so much.

They finished lunch and spent another hour walking around the park, visiting the various vendors and stopping to listen to a woman who played "America the Beautiful" on a hammered dulcimer.

"I'm walked out," Mrs. Shepherd said as they approached the food court again.

"Time for us to head home," Mr. Shepherd said.

"You're not staying for the fireworks?" Tammy asked.

"We can see great fireworks from our backyard in Junction," Mrs. Shepherd said. "Maybe not as spectacular as here in the mountains, but when they're done, we can go right to bed." She laughed. "I can see the idea is appalling to you, but when you get to be our age, it's a plus."

They each hugged Vince goodbye, then surprised Tammy by embracing her too. "Your parents are such nice people," Tammy said when they were gone.

"They are." He slipped his arm around her shoulders. "But it's good to be alone with you too."

"Was the water in the dunk tank cold?" she asked.

"Icy." He grimaced.

"It was for a good cause." She patted his chest. "And you looked good up there."

"That was your brother who tried to take me down toward the end, wasn't it?"

"Yes, that was Mitch. And the woman who got you afterwards is his girlfriend, Elisabeth."

"Elisabeth who?"

She frowned. "I don't remember." She or Mitch must have said, but the name escaped her. "She's from Nebraska, I think. Though I guess she's decided to stay here."

"Where in Nebraska?"

"I don't remember. Why?"

"She looked familiar."

"You've probably seen her around town. She's the kind of woman men notice."

"Nah. Not my type." He grinned. "I prefer curly-haired blondes."

They spotted Gage and Travis Walker, and Vince waved. The two law enforcement officers joined them. "I saw you at the dunking booth," Gage said. "You got soaked."

"Next year, I'm going to lobby for them to fill the tank with warm water," Vince said.

"It wouldn't be nearly as fun then."

"You can both pick your vehicles up from our impound

lot tomorrow," Travis said. "We weren't able to get a great deal of information off of them, unfortunately."

"I'll have to call a wrecker to haul mine away," Vince said. "I wish you could find who did that and make them pay for the repairs."

"No more love letters from V?" Gage asked.

"None," Vince said. Which wasn't a lie, Tammy reminded herself. Gage hadn't asked about phone calls.

She waited until the lawmen were some distance away before she asked, "Have you had any more phone calls?"

"No. I'm hoping we're done with all that. Whoever it was has moved on to bothering someone else."

She slipped her hand in his and they walked on, their lighter mood from earlier subdued. But they had a whole afternoon to regain that lighter feeling. And fireworks tonight, which never failed to lift her spirits.

"I need to stop here for a minute," she said when she spotted the restrooms. She slipped away to the ladies' room, leaving him waiting outside. When she emerged a few minutes later, Vince was talking to a dark-haired woman—one of the other search and rescue volunteers, Tammy remembered.

At Tammy's approach, the woman looked up, then hurried away. Tammy stared after her. "Who was that?" she asked.

"Bethany Ames. She's with search and rescue."

"Why did she run away when she saw me?"

Vince made a face. "I think she was embarrassed. She asked if I wanted to watch the fireworks with her tonight. I told her I was going with you. She stammered an apology and left."

Amused, she slipped her hand in his. "I didn't realize I had competition."

"No competition. Bethany isn't my type."

"She's cute."

"Yeah, but…she's a little too intense, you know? Something about her puts me off."

"How long have you known her?" Tammy asked.

"Not long. She just moved to town and joined the group."

Was it a coincidence that this woman had moved to town and taken an interest in Vince at the same time someone had started harassing him?

"What is it?" Vince asked.

"Nothing?"

"Are you sure? You look worried."

"It's nothing." No sense worrying Vince. She would do a little digging on her own to see what she could find out about Bethany Ames before she said anything. "Let's go back to the music stage," she urged. "There's supposed to be a bluegrass band there at four. I've heard good things about them."

The band deserved the praise she had heard, and she and Vince were soon tapping their toes and nodding their heads in time to the lively music. She was so engrossed that she didn't realize Vince had received a phone call until he moved away. One look at his expression set her heart racing, and she hurried to his side.

His eyes met hers, stricken. "It's my dad," he told her, then spoke into the phone again. "Are you and Mom okay? All right. I'll be there as soon as I can."

He ended the call, then pulled Tammy away from the crowd that had gathered to listen to the music. "My parents got home, and there were fire trucks lining their street. The fire was at their house."

Chapter Eighteen

"I'm coming with you to your parents'," Tammy said. It wasn't a question.

"You don't have to do that." He dug his keys out from his jeans pocket. Was there anything else he needed to do before he left?

"I want to come," she said.

"What about the fireworks photos?"

"Russ can take them. I want to be with you. And your parents."

He grabbed her hand and squeezed it. "Thanks. That means a lot."

He thought she understood what he was saying. After Valerie had disappeared, Vince had been left alone, his parents distracted by grief. It became a point of pride to get through things alone. Not having to do that anymore was a special gift.

They started walking toward his car. "Dad said the fire is out and most of the damage is to one upstairs bedroom," he said. "The rest of the house is okay except for smoke damage. He and Mom are waiting for the fire department to give them the green light to go inside."

"Do they have any idea what started it?" Tammy asked.

"Dad didn't say. The house is at least as old as I am. Maybe there was a fault in the electrical wiring?"

They didn't say much on the drive to Junction. Vince gripped the steering wheel and forced himself to keep within ten miles of the speed limit, willing the time to pass more quickly. His dad had said there wasn't a lot of damage, but what did that mean? Would his parents be able to remain in the house, or did they need somewhere else to stay? Was the fire an accident or deliberate? And why was all this happening now?

A lone fire truck sat at the curb when they arrived. A firefighter and a Junction police officer met them at the end of the drive, where Vince's parents also waited. "We're confident the fire is out," the firefighter said. "But call if you see any more smoke or flames."

"I don't understand," Mr. Shepherd said. "How did the fire start?"

The police officer introduced himself as Sergeant Fisk. "Where were you today, Mr. Shepherd?" he asked.

"We were in Eagle Mountain, visiting our son and attending the Fourth of July celebration," Dad said.

"Does anyone else live in the house besides you and your wife?"

"No."

"Do you know of anyone who might want to harm you and your wife or your home?"

"No. What are you talking about? Are you saying the fire was deliberately set?"

"The blaze started in the upstairs back bedroom," Fisk said. "Whose bedroom is that?"

"No one's," Dad said.

"That was our daughter, Valerie's, room," Mom said, her voice strained.

"Where is your daughter now?" Sergeant Fisk asked.

Her face crumpled and tears slid down her cheeks. Dad

pulled her close. "Our daughter disappeared fifteen years ago," he said. "We don't know where she is."

Fisk looked back toward the house. From this angle, it appeared undamaged. "Did someone set the fire intentionally?" Vince asked.

"It looks that way," Fisk said. He turned back to Vince. "You're the son?"

"Yes. I'm Vince Shepherd."

The officer turned to Tammy. "And you are?"

"Tammy Patterson. I'm Vince's friend."

"You two were in Eagle Mountain this morning also?"

"Yes," Vince said. "Tammy was taking photographs for the paper, and I worked a fundraising booth for the local search and rescue group. How did the fire start?"

The firefighter spoke. "Someone piled a bunch of papers—pages torn from books, from the looks of things— and set the fire in the middle of the bed. The neighbor whose backyard adjoins this one saw the smoke and called 911." He turned to Mr. and Mrs. Shepherd. "You can return to the house, but don't go into that bedroom. You'll need to have a restoration company see about cleaning it up. There's a lot of smoke damage, and we can't be sure there isn't structural damage from the flames."

Mom moaned, and Dad tightened his arm around her. "Did anyone see somebody near the house this morning?" he asked.

"We spoke with the neighbors," Fisk said. "No one remembers anything unusual. Have any of you noticed anything out of the ordinary recently?"

"No," Dad said. Mom shook her head.

Vince felt Tammy tense beside him, but he said nothing.

They waited until the firefighter and Sergeant Fisk had left before they went into the house. Vince smelled smoke when they entered, but the scent wasn't as strong as he had expected. He followed his mother and father up the stairs, Tammy behind him. The closer they walked to the bedroom, the more intense the odor of smoke.

They halted outside the bedroom. His dad pushed open the door to reveal the smoke and soot-blackened remains of a little girl's bedroom. Parts of the pink comforter on the bed were still intact, though the center was a black hole. Half a dozen books lay scattered at the foot of the bed, some splayed with spines showing, others with charred pages. Black outlines showed where flames had charred the walls, and everything was sodden.

Mom turned away, sobbing, and fled past them down the hall. Vince started to go after her, but his dad took hold of his arm. "Let her go," he said. "She needs a little time alone." He closed the door, and the three of them returned to the living room.

"Why didn't you tell the police about the notes Vince and I have received, and the messages left on Vince's and my vehicles?" Tammy asked.

"Those things happened in Eagle Mountain," Dad said. "We don't know that they have anything to do with us."

"Except the person who wrote the notes signed them with a V and implied they were Valerie." Tammy's voice was gentle but insistent.

Dad sat heavily on the sofa. "Why would Valerie destroy her own room?" he asked. "And those notes—why would she blame any of us for what happened to her?"

Vince sat in an armchair facing the sofa. Tammy perched on the arm of the chair. "Why didn't you and Mom ever have Valerie declared dead?" he asked. He had never voiced the question before, not wanting to cause his parents more pain. But he wondered if they knew something he didn't.

"We considered it," Dad said. "But we didn't want to give up hope."

"Did anything happen to give you hope?" Tammy asked.

He didn't answer. Vince cleared his throat. "You mentioned seeing a young woman in a casino who looked like Valerie."

Dad sighed, his gaze focused on the rug. "There were two phone calls, years apart. Once, the person—a female—just said, 'Help.' Another time all she said was 'Dad?' and then hung up before I could answer. I'm sure they were just people being cruel, but we always wondered, what if they really were Valerie?"

Vince's stomach rolled, and he feared he might be sick. Rescue work had schooled him to be strong when faced with others' pain, but broken limbs and gashed heads were nothing compared to seeing his father tortured this way.

"You must have tried to find her over the years," Tammy said.

"We did. We hired private detectives twice, but they never came up with anything. They tried to find the camper that was in the mountains the day we were but never found a trace of him either."

"I didn't know that," Vince said. "About the detectives, I mean."

Dad glanced at him. "You had your own life to lead," he said. "We didn't want to burden you with our concerns."

"What will you do now?" Tammy asked.

"We'll get someone in to fix the house." He looked at Vince again. "And before you ask, no, we won't move. Your mother, especially, would never leave this place."

"Because Valerie might come home." Tammy's voice was scarcely above a whisper, but it was loud in the still room.

"Yes. When you have children of your own one day, you'll

understand. We can never give up hope. No matter how much it hurts."

When would the hurting stop? Vince wondered. Sure, the pain of grief and the memory of a smiling little girl who had once been part of their lives would always be part of them. But this new pain, of a wound constantly reopened, when would that end? How could he make it end?

Fifteen years ago.

"WE'RE GOING TO need to give you a new name."

She looked up at the man who stood over her. The man with the friendly smile who had brought her to this place—a place she didn't know. The smile frightened her now, though she didn't know why. He hadn't done anything to hurt her. "Can you think of a name you would like to go by now?" he asked.

"Why do I have to have a new name?" she asked. "Why can't I go home?"

The man—he had told her his name was Paul—squatted down so he could look at her directly. He had dark eyes. They looked all black, like a cartoon character's. They had frightened her at first, but she was getting used to them. "I explained this already," he said. "Your mom and dad didn't want you anymore. They were going to leave you up there in the mountains to die, until I agreed to take you instead."

"Why didn't they want me?" Her heart beat so fast it hurt at the idea. "They said they loved me."

"They were liars." He shrugged. "People are, sometimes. You'll learn that as you get older. They thought they'd be happier with just one kid, and they decided to keep your brother because he's a boy. Some people feel that way. But I don't." He reached out and gently stroked her head. "I always wanted a little girl like you."

She began to cry. He let her. They sat like that for a long time, him stroking her hair. "It's going to be all right," he said. "You can help me with my work."

She sniffed and tried to control her tears. She didn't like the way crying felt. If she helped him, maybe he would let her talk her parents. If she talked to them, she could get them to take her back. Whatever she had done to upset them, she could make up for it. She just had to convince Paul to let her see them again. "What kind of work?" she asked.

"People give me money to invest," he said. "You'll be good at persuading them to give me the money. You're a pretty child, and people will like you. Sometimes I'll ask you to talk to people while I take things they don't need anymore. Things we can use. You're smart. I could tell that just by watching you there at the camp."

"I got all As on my last report card," she said.

"I knew you were smart," he said. "I'm good at reading people. I'll teach you how to read them too. The two of us will make a fine team." He stood at last. "We'll be good together. You'll see. After a while you won't even think about your old family anymore."

I'll never forget my family, she thought. And that had turned out to be true. But over the years, she saw them differently. She saw them the way Paul saw them. It was an ugly view, but then, much of life was ugly. Paul had taught her that. She had learned a great deal from him. She had learned that a smart, daring person could get whatever she wanted from people who weren't as smart—money, admiration, sex.

Revenge.

Chapter Nineteen

"Should we tell the sheriff we think the fire at your parents' home might have been started by V?" Tammy asked as she and Vince made the drive back to Eagle Mountain.

"We don't have any proof at all that V started the fire," he said.

"Except that the fire was in Valerie's room, and V has connected herself with Valerie."

"That isn't proof, though, is it? And Junction isn't in Travis's jurisdiction. Not even close. Plus, my dad refuses to say anything to the Junction police about our troubles with V. He doesn't want to believe they're connected."

"Then what are we going to do?"

"I don't think we can do anything but wait for her to make another move. Travis has already admitted whoever this is hasn't left much evidence for them to trace."

Goose bumps rose on Tammy's arms, and she hugged herself, trying to fend off the sudden chill. "It feels like she's getting more dangerous—that attack on me and now this fire."

"The attack on you was terrible," he said. "And the fire was frightening and destructive, but she didn't try to burn down the whole house."

"If that neighbor hadn't seen the smoke and called 911, the whole house might have burned."

"I'm worried she might hurt my parents," Vince said. "But they won't move out of the house, even temporarily."

"They can't believe Valerie would hurt them."

"But someone pretending to be Valerie might. I tried to tell Dad that, but he won't listen."

"My mom never listens to me either," she said. "We're still kids to them, and they're still our parents. The police in Junction are still investigating the arson. Maybe they'll get lucky and find a witness or something else that leads them to V. In the meantime, you and I will have to keep our eyes open."

"It's not like either of us have the skills or the time to investigate this full-time," he said. "And I don't have money to hire a private investigator." He pounded his fist against the steering wheel. "It's so frustrating."

"It is," she agreed. "But we'll get through this. I have an idea we can try. I'll have to talk to Russ and see if he will agree, but I think he will."

"What's that?"

"I'm thinking I could do another story for the paper, about Valerie. V's version of what happened that day is so different from what actually happened, a new story might draw her out again."

"'Draw her out,' how? What if she tries to kill someone? What if she tries to kill you?"

Her stomach knotted with fear. "I'll be careful," she said. "I won't go anywhere alone. And it will be worth it if we can draw her out."

"But how are we going to catch her? What if your article just results in another taunting letter or phone call, or a sneak attack?"

Tammy chewed on her thumbnail, thinking. "We'll have to set a trap," she said. She sat up straight. "I know! We can say there's going to be a memorial to honor Valerie and keep awareness of her alive. In the park. The public is invited. She'll be sure to come. We can alert the sheriff, and they can have a deputy there. We can watch for anyone behaving suspiciously."

"It might work," Vince said. "Do you think the sheriff will agree?"

"We can ask. And the memorial itself will be news enough that I won't have any trouble getting Russ to run a small piece."

"If it's a memorial, we'll need to tell my parents. They'll want to come."

"They can come. But don't tell them it's a trap for V. Just say it's something you wanted to do to honor your sister. Tell them it was my idea, if that helps."

"Are people going to think it's strange we're doing this now, when we haven't done anything for fifteen years?"

"I don't think there's any timeline for these things," she said. "It might even help your parents to have a public ceremony like this. There will be other people who attend who remember Valerie, teachers and others who knew her. They'll know they're not alone in their grief."

"Like the funeral we never had." He nodded. "I think it will be a good thing—and if it helps stop V from harassing us, even better."

"You can talk to your parents tomorrow. I'll check with the sheriff and find out if we need a permit to hold the memorial in the park."

"It feels right to be doing something," Vince said. "Instead of sitting back, waiting for the next bad thing to happen."

VINCE WAS SURE his parents would resist the idea of a memorial for Valerie. He would have to work to persuade them, or even go through with the plan without their blessing. But once again, they surprised him. Instead of bursting into tears, as he had expected, his mother had responded with enthusiasm. "I have some wonderful pictures we can display at the memorial," she said. "And there's a poem I came across, not long after she went missing, that I found meaningful. I don't think I could read it out loud in front of people, but perhaps you could. Or maybe Tammy?"

"That sounds great, Mom. Tammy's arranging things with the city for us to be allowed to hold the memorial in the park."

"I used to think about doing something like this in the mountains, at the place we saw her last," his mom said. "But I suppose the park is more practical. Much easier for people to get to. Thank you for doing this."

"It wasn't my idea. It was Tammy's."

"She's a lovely young woman." His mother fixed him with the look that made him feel like a boy being quizzed on whether or not he had completed his homework. "Are things serious between you two?" she asked.

"We don't want to rush things," he said. Though the truth was, they were as good as living together, with Tammy spending every night at his place and most of her belongings there. He thought soon he would formally ask her to move in full-time, with a change of address and everything. The idea made his heart race a little, but not in a bad way.

After getting his parents on board, the next step was a meeting with the sheriff. He and Tammy went to Travis's office and laid out their proposal for catching V. "She associates so strongly with Valerie, I don't think she'll be able to stay away from the service," Tammy said. "Eagle Mountain is a small enough community we ought to able to spot someone new or out of place."

"I can't arrest someone for being a stranger," Travis said.

"And grief can make people behave in odd ways. That's not a crime either."

"But you can watch them, and if they do cause trouble, you can have a deputy there to put a stop to it," she said.

"All right," Travis agreed. "But you have to promise to let us handle any incidents. You focus on the memorial."

"I promise," Tammy said, and Vince agreed.

Travis sat back in his chair. "I understand there was a fire at your parents' house," he said. "In your sister's old bedroom."

"How did you hear about that?" Vince asked, unable to hide his alarm.

"I have friends with the Junction police. They called to verify that you and your parents were in Eagle Mountain the day of the fire."

"They were checking our alibis?" Vince's voice rose.

"It's routine in an arson investigation. They don't have any leads as to who set the fire. Do you think it was V?"

"It could have been," Vince admitted. "It's one reason we planned this memorial. I don't like her getting close to my parents. She's already hurt Tammy. I don't want her to hurt anyone else."

Travis turned to Tammy. "What do you plan to say in your article for the paper?"

"I'm just going to announce the memorial, say anyone who remembers Valerie is invited and give a brief outline of the circumstances of her disappearance."

"Play up the loving family who never stopped searching for her," Travis said. "That contradicts V's story that Valerie's disappearance was somehow orchestrated by the family. She may feel she has to show up to refute that."

"I thought we could have a portion of the memorial service where people can stand up and offer their memories of Valerie," she said. "Maybe V will have something to say."

"We could get lucky." Travis stood. "I'll have a couple of deputies at the service," he said. "Let me know if you need anything else."

THE DAY OF Valerie's memorial was hot and sunny. Vince's parents had insisted on a large flower arrangement, and a couple of Valerie's former teachers and a family friend had also ordered arrangements, which Tammy grouped around a series of enlarged photos of the little girl. Though she and Vince were not identical twins, the resemblance was definitely there, and one photo Mrs. Shepherd had provided showed the children together, arms around each other, grinning for the camera with such happiness it made Tammy's heart hurt.

"There are more people here than I thought there would be," Mrs. Shepherd said as they watched people fill the folding chairs they had set out. Latecomers stood around the chairs, all facing the small platform with the flowers and photographs. Tammy scanned the gathering, hoping to spot anyone who seemed out of place or who was behaving strangely. But no one stood out.

At two o'clock sharp, Tammy moved to the microphone set up in front of the platform. "On behalf of the Shepherd family, I want to thank you all for coming this afternoon," she said. "We are gathered to honor a beloved daughter, sister and friend. Valerie Shepherd vanished from our lives fifteen years ago, but she has never been forgotten. And the family has never stopped looking for her."

She looked out over the crowd and faltered for a moment when she recognized Mitch and Elisabeth, seated on the back row of chairs. She had mentioned she was planning this event for the family, and this show of support touched her. It wasn't the kind of thing Mitch would ever have done on his own, so it must be Elisabeth's influence. She would be sure to thank her later.

She looked down at her notes. "To start, I want to read a poem at the request of Valerie's mother." She read the poem, a sentimental piece about the joy a little girl brings to the family. By the time she was done, Mrs. Shepherd was wiping away tears, as were many others in the crowd.

"Now we'll have an opportunity for anyone who would like to share their memories of Valerie. Her brother, Vince, will start."

Vince, dressed in dark slacks and a blue dress shirt, sleeves rolled up and collar open, moved to the microphone. Tammy spotted a number of his fellow search and rescue volunteers in the crowd, some of whom must have been involved in the original search for Valerie. Bethany Ames was there. Did that mean she was Valerie?

Vince glanced at a note card in his hand, then cleared his throat and spoke: "When I think of my sister, Valerie, I think of her courage. We were twins, but she got most of the bravery in the family. She truly wasn't afraid of anything—spiders, heights, deep water, going fast on a mountain bike—all the things that made me nervous never fazed her.

"I remember once, we were riding our bikes in the woods behind our house. Our usual route took us over a ditch, where someone had laid down a couple of boards to make it possible to ride over. But on this day, spring snowmelt had the water in the ditch raging, and had washed the boards downstream. I told Valerie we would have to turn around and go back home the long way, but she insisted we could jump our bikes over the water.

"I looked at that rushing water and my other big fear—of drowning—had me almost paralyzed. I told Valerie I couldn't do it, but she insisted I could. She backed her bike up a hill, then pedaled furiously down it, gaining speed. When she reached the edge of the ditch, she yanked up on the handle-bars and sailed over the gap with room to spare. She wheeled around, shouting in triumph, and told me it was my turn.

"I could have turned around and ridden home alone, but I would have had to live with the shame—and the constant taunts from her—that she had beat me. So I backed my bike up the hill, pedaled with everything I had and held my breath as my bike cleared that gap. Valerie was thrilled, congrat-ulating me and telling me she had known all along that I could do it. I was just relieved that I had survived unscathed.

"After she was gone, I realized how much I had relied on her to lead the way. It was a hard lesson to learn, but I'm a better man for it. I learned that I needed to be brave enough for both of us."

Tammy watched the faces of those in the crowd as he spoke. Many people were smiling, some nodding their heads. But no one looked angry or upset by the story. Deputies Jamie Douglas and Dwight Prentice stood on either side of the crowd, assessing the attendees but not reacting as if they had spotted anything concerning.

Vince left the microphone and returned to his seat on the front row between his mother and Tammy. Others took turns speaking—two different teachers spoke about how smart Valerie was. Her former soccer coach spoke about her talent for the sport and cheerful attitude. Mr. and Mrs. Shepherd each shared memories of their little girl, their voices break-ing as they painted a picture of a cheerful and loved child.

And then it was over. Members of the crowd moved for-ward to speak with the family while others drifted away. Tammy looked for Mitch and Elisabeth, but they had al-ready left. It didn't matter. She could thank them later for being there.

Jamie came to stand beside her. "Did you see anyone out of place?" she asked.

"No," Tammy admitted. "Did you?"

"No. Everyone was quiet and respectful. I didn't see anything off."

Dwight Prentice walked up. "Everything seems okay," he said.

"I guess our plan didn't work," Vince said.

"It was still a beautiful memorial," Jamie said. "I didn't know your sister, but it sounds like she was a great kid."

"She was." Vince took a deep breath and blew it out. "I'm glad we did this, even if we didn't catch V. We should have done it years ago."

Tammy slipped her arm in his. "I'm glad we did it too. It helped me to know Valerie and your family better."

They helped his parents load the flowers and pictures to take back to their home in Junction, which Mr. Shepherd reported was already in the process of being repaired.

Tammy and Vince were walking across the park toward the lot where they had left the Escape when Vince's text alert sounded. He pulled out his phone. "It's a search and rescue call," he said, and scrolled through the message. "Hikers reported an injured man at the base of the cliffs north of Dixon Pass." He met her eyes. "I should go."

"Do you need to change clothes and grab your gear?" she asked.

"I keep a change of clothes and a gear bag in the car," he said.

"Then go."

"I can drop you off at the condo," he said.

"I want to walk over and visit my mother," she said. "I'll get her to drive me to your condo."

"You should start thinking of it as *our* condo," he said. "You're spending all your time there."

"I am, but I don't want to presume."

He took her by the shoulders. "I like having you live with me. I think you should go ahead and move in. Permanently."

She grinned, a little numb and a lot excited. "Yes. Let's do it."

"We'll iron out the details later." He kissed her on the lips. "Right now, I need to go." He started to open the car, then stopped. "Be careful. V is still out there somewhere."

"It'll be fine," she said. "It's broad daylight, and there are tons of people around. When I get to the condo I'll lock myself in. I promise. And you be careful too. Don't fall off a cliff or anything."

"I won't."

She waved goodbye and walked the three blocks to her mother's house. But her mother wasn't home. Neither was Mitch. Disappointed but undeterred, Tammy pulled her bicycle from the garage and set off toward the condo by the river.

Chapter Twenty

"It's a miracle anyone spotted this guy down there," SAR volunteer Harper Stanick said as she and a dozen other volunteers stood on the narrow shoulder of the highway, staring down into the canyon below.

"If those two guys hadn't decided to climb the cliff today, no telling how long he would have lain down there," Tony Meissner said. He looked around. "Where are they, anyway?"

"I sent them on their way," Deputy Ryker Vernon said. "We've got their names and contact info. They're locals, so they shouldn't be hard to get hold of if we need to talk to them later."

"They were pretty shook up," Deputy Declan Owen said. "They said they have no idea who the guy is. I think they were being truthful."

Danny lowered the binoculars he had been using to study the figure of the man below. "I can't tell if he's breathing or not," he said. "And there's a lot of blood. We need to get down there, ASAP."

"The descent is straightforward enough," Tony said. "But bringing him out is going to be pretty technical."

"Sheri, you and Tony go down first," Danny said. "Hannah, you're the medical on scene. Caleb, you and Vince up for following them down?"

"Sure thing," Caleb said.

"Of course," Vince answered. He had trained half a dozen times on similar climbs. He had never had any trouble and was anxious to try his skills in a real rescue situation.

Danny assigned other volunteers to help with the ropes and provide backup as needed. Ryker and Declan had already closed the road to traffic. Now they set about establishing a landing zone for a medical helicopter, should one be needed.

"Any idea how he ended up down there?" Vince asked as he and Caleb gathered their equipment.

"Solo climbing?" Caleb suggested. "Not a good idea, but people do it."

"There aren't any ropes, or even anchors at the top," Ryan said.

"Maybe he set an anchor and it pulled out." Eldon made a face. "If that happened, he's done for."

"No sense speculating," Tony said. "We'll find out when we get there."

The quartet carried their gear to the edge of the canyon above where the body lay. Tony and Sheri decided on the best place to set anchors, then directed the others in laying out the ropes, carabiners, brake bars and other equipment they would use to lower themselves to the man in the canyon and eventually bring a litter up to the top again.

They were all aware of the need to reach the man as soon as possible, but no one rushed. Safety required precision and attention to detail. They wanted the man to live, but not at the expense of any one of them.

Sheri started down first; then Tony set out, ten feet to the left of her. Experienced climbers and competitors on the climbing circuit, they descended smoothly and swiftly. The canyon walls were jagged but stable, providing plenty of hand- and footholds when necessary, though the two were able to glide down long stretches of the wall. Tony landed first, followed seconds later by Sheri. The others watched from the top as they surrounded the crumpled figure on the ground.

"He's alive," Sheri radioed. "Nonresponsive. He's lost a lot of blood. There's a head wound, but I don't see any ropes or a harness or other gear."

There was a pause, the crackle of the radio; then Tony transmitted: "This was no climbing accident. This guy's been shot. Right shoulder. He's got probable broken bones and the head injury. Get that chopper over here. We need to bring this guy up ASAP."

"Hannah, you ready to go?" Danny asked.

"I'm there." Hannah was already at the edge of the canyon, poised to begin the descent.

"Caleb, you and Vince take the litter and the vacuum mattress, and a helmet for the injured man. Ryan and Eldon, you set the high-angle rigging to bring up the litter. I'm calling for the chopper."

As soon as Hannah reached the bottom, Caleb and Vince set out, the litter and other equipment distributed between them, along with extra lines that would eventually be used to haul the patient in the litter to the surface. Eldon and Ryan took the belay position at the top and lowered them down the cliff.

Vince focused on keeping untangled and steady, and the descent happened so quickly he scarcely had time to be nervous. When he had unclipped from the line, he hurried to the huddle around the injured man.

"Get that mattress down here, and we'll shift him onto it," Tony directed.

"I've got the IV in," Hannah said. "I'll start a bag of saline. Somebody unpack a few chemical heat packs to help keep him warm." She keyed the radio and rattled off numbers for the man's pulse, blood pressure and oxygen levels.

Vince leaned in to get a closer look at the man. Maroon bloodstains painted his slacks and dress shirt—not clothing for a climb or a hike in the mountains. "Do you think someone shot him and pushed him down here?" he asked.

Tony looked up. "Either they pushed him or he fell."

"Do we know who he is?" Caleb asked.

"His wallet has an ID for Mitchell Patterson," Sheri said. "Do either of you know him?"

Vince stared at the man's battered shape, stunned. He never would have recognized Tammy's brother, he was so bruised and swollen. "That's Tammy's brother," he said.

"Tammy Patterson?" Hannah looked over her shoulder at them. "Of course. Mitch Patterson, the real estate agent." She turned back to him. "How did he end up down here?"

"That's for the sheriff to find out." Tony stood. "Let's get him in the litter and up to that helicopter."

They worked together to slide Mitch's body—which was fitted with the IV, an oxygen mask, and various splints and bandages—onto the vacuum mattress, which was then inflated to fit tightly around him, acting as a full-body splint. This was then placed in the litter. He was strapped in, along with heat packs, blankets, the IV fluids and oxygen tank.

The litter was attached to lines that hung down from a tripod at the canyon rim that helped to keep the litter suspended away from the canyon walls. Then Sheri and Tony began the arduous process of ascending the canyon walls while guiding the litter up between them.

Vince stood with Hannah and Caleb and watched the ascent. While the lines from the tripod would support most of the weight of the litter, the two climbers needed to hold it steady while navigating their own journey to the top.

"There's the chopper," Hannah said.

Vince listened and heard the faint throb of helicopter rotors. "Do you think he'll make it?" he asked.

She pulled off her latex gloves and tucked them in the pocket of her jacket. "He has a chance. I don't think he had been down here long when we got to him. We were able to stabilize him and ward off shock. But he has a lot of injuries. Probably some internal ones I wasn't able to assess. I couldn't tell you what his chances are."

When Mitch was safely to the top of the canyon, along with Sheri and Tony, Caleb and Vince helped Hannah gather the medical equipment and other supplies. They packed everything away. Hannah and Caleb ascended first, leaving Vince for last. He took out his phone and stared at the screen, even though he knew he had no signal here. He would need to contact Tammy and let her know what had happened to her brother.

But what had happened? Who had shot him and left him to die in this remote spot? He and his girlfriend had attended Valerie's memorial service a few hours ago—though now it seemed like days. The shooting must have happened shortly after that.

Fear lanced through him as another thought registered. Elisabeth was probably with Mitch when he was shot. What had happened to her?

TAMMY COASTED THE bicycle up to the front door of the condo and dismounted. The ride had energized her. Maybe she would start riding her bike to work. She wondered what Russ would think of that.

She took out her keys and unlocked the door, then wheeled the bicycle in ahead of her and left it against the wall in the front hall. She would need to find a better place to park it, but they would figure out something.

"Hello, Tammy. I was wondering what took you so long."

She froze, then slowly turned around to face Elisabeth. Or rather, she registered that the voice was Elisabeth's, but her gaze fixed on the gun in the woman's hand and refused to look away.

"Where's Vince?" Elisabeth asked.

"He had a search and rescue call. A climber fell in a canyon, up on Dixon Pass."

Elisabeth's laughter was another shock. "Oh, that's rich," she crowed. "Not what I had planned at all, but this might be even better."

Tammy forced her gaze away from the gun, but the expression on Elisabeth's face did nothing to calm her. The other woman was as sleek and put together as ever, with her long hair swept back in a low ponytail and the nails that rested against the gun sporting a perfect French manicure. But her eyes were dilated, her mouth fixed in a rictus of a smile. "How did you get in here?" Tammy asked.

"The first time I visited the manager's apartment, when I rented my place, I swiped a master key. I knew it would come in handy one day."

"What are you doing here?" Tammy tried to sound strong and in control. "And put away that gun."

"Who do you think you are, that you can tell me what to do? Now, get over there on that couch and sit down." She gestured toward the sofa with her free hand.

Tammy did as she was told, moving sideways so that her back was never to the other woman. "Where's Mitch?" she asked. "I saw the two of you at the memorial service."

"You didn't think I'd miss my own memorial service, did you?"

Twin Jeopardy

Elisabeth was V. Tammy had figured that out when she saw the gun in her hand. But did that also mean she was Valerie? "Where's Mitch?" she asked again.

"I left him at the bottom of a canyon, up on Dixon Pass. But apparently, my brother is helping to get him out. Or more probably, he's retrieving his body." She sat in a chair facing the sofa, the gun aimed at the middle of Tammy's chest. "That's inconvenient, but it will give us time to talk."

The idea that Mitch might be dead hit Tammy like a blow to the stomach. She wanted to protest that that couldn't be true, but she recognized the fruitlessness of arguing. She pushed the idea away entirely. She wouldn't think about Mitch right now. She had to focus on Valerie, and on keeping her from pulling the trigger. "What happened to you?" she asked. "That day on the camping trip, when you were ten?"

"I knew you'd have questions. I guess that's the reporter in you. Too bad you weren't around when I went missing. You strike me as someone who might actually have ferreted out the truth."

"What is the truth?" Tammy asked.

"I've been trying to tell you for weeks. My family—my mother and father and Vince—decided they didn't want me anymore. They were going to leave me up on that mountain to die. Instead, a man who was camping nearby offered to take care of me."

"The man kidnapped you," Tammy said.

"He didn't kidnap me. He did me a favor. I would have died without him."

Her agitation—and the way the gun shook in her hand—made Tammy nervous. She had to resist the impulse to argue. "What was the man's name?" she asked.

"Paul. Paul Rollins."

"And you're Elisabeth Rollins."

"Paul chose the name for me. Much better than Valerie."

"Where is Paul now?" Should Tammy expect him to walk through the door at any moment?

"He's dead. With him gone, I didn't have anyone left. Then I remembered my other family. The one who abandoned me."

Tammy bit her lip to keep from arguing that the Shepherds had not abandoned their daughter. Time to change the subject again. She needed to keep Valerie off-balance. "What happened with Mitch?" she asked.

"I needed him out of the way so I could take care of Vince and my parents." She crossed her legs and propped the grip of the handgun on her knee, her finger within easy reach of the trigger. "I would have liked to keep him around longer, at least until I had drained off more of his money. I thought I would have time to access all of his accounts before anyone discovered his body, but that may not be the case now."

"He loved you," Tammy said.

"So have the others." Her smile brightened. "I guess I'm just a very lovable person."

"I don't understand how Paul was able to keep you a secret all these years," Tammy said. "People were looking for you. Your parents hired a private detective. There were appeals in the media."

"Lies, all of it. If they were looking as hard as they said, they would have found me. Paul changed my name, sure, and he took me to a fancy salon and got me a good haircut—my first one. But the rest of me was just the same. It's not like we were living in a cave in the middle of nowhere. We lived in a beautiful house. We took vacations."

"What about school?"

"I was homeschooled. Paul had been a teacher, once upon a time. He taught me what I needed to know to help him in his business."

"What kind of business was that?"

That overly bright grin again. "Paul liked to say we taught people important financial lessons. We taught people to be more careful with their money."

"You conned people," Tammy guessed.

"*Con* sounds so crass. What we did required more finesse. We persuaded people to trust us. Most of them did."

"Is that why you're here now? Because you want money?"

"I have money, and I always know how to get more. No, I'm here for a different kind of payback."

Tammy swallowed hard. The gun, and the fact that Valerie had admitted to killing Mitch, indicated the payback could be a fatal one. "I'm not part of your family," she said. "Why waste your time with me?"

"Because Vince *loooves* you." She drew out the word. "The first time I saw you together, I knew it. He didn't care about me, his twin, but he's all gaga for you. Hurting you will hurt him. I thought at first that beating you up would be enough. You put up quite a fight, by the way. I can admire that, even if it made things inconvenient for me. But it also made me realize that a beating wasn't going to be enough. Vince can watch you die, then I'll kill him. It will be perfect."

Tammy choked back a moan. "What about your parents?" she asked. She didn't want more horrible details, but she needed to keep Valerie talking.

"I'll get them next, but no hurry. I won't have to sneak up on them like I did you and Vince. They'll be happy to open the door for their long-lost little girl. Then I can take my time deciding how to put an end to them and all their lies about truly loving me."

Tammy heard the hurt behind the hatred. What had Paul done to this young woman to damage her so much?

But she couldn't let sympathy blind her to the danger she was in. And Vince. Could she find a way to warn him before he came home and walked into his own death sentence?

Chapter Twenty-One

It was after seven when Vince unlocked the Escape parked at search and rescue headquarters. He had tried calling Tammy as soon as he picked up a phone signal, but the call had gone to voice mail after six rings. Maybe she was in the shower or busy with something else.

It was better if he gave her the message about her brother in person. Or maybe she already knew. That might explain why she hadn't answered the phone. She might be with her mother. Vince had told Declan and Ryker about Elisabeth as soon as he reached the top of the canyon, and they had radioed the information to the sheriff and started the search for her. They would have reached out to Mrs. Patterson and Tammy too.

"Vince, wait up!" He looked up and let out a groan when he saw Bethany jogging toward him.

"I don't have time to talk now," he said.

She stopped in front of him. "This won't take long. I just want to apologize for being so, well, awkward around you." She studied the ground between them. "I came to town to make a fresh start, right? I was trying to be all independent, going after what I wanted and that kind of thing? And I thought you were cute and nice and would be a fun date. But I should have realized you were already involved. I was so embarrassed when I found out you were already with someone. But I just wanted you to know I won't bother you anymore. And no hard feelings—I hope."

"Sure. No hard feelings." She looked so sad, standing there with her head down. Harmless, and probably lonely too. "Are you okay?"

She looked up, a forced smiled on her lips. "I'm fine." She shrugged. "Being alone in a new place is hard, but I'm starting to make friends."

"Count me as one of them," he said. "Me and Tammy."

The smile became more genuine. "Thanks." She took a step back. "I'll let you go now." She turned and hurried away, this time with her head up.

Vince drove to his condo and parked. Tammy had left the outside light on for him. Keys in hand, he moved toward the door. But it wasn't locked. Not good. Maybe she had forgotten in her distress over her brother, but with V still at large, it wasn't safe to leave the condo unsecured.

The hallway was dark. He left his jacket and pack on the hooks by the door, then almost fell over a bicycle. What was that doing there?

"Tammy?" he called.

"Vince, don't— *Ahhh!*"

He sprinted toward the living room but skidded to a stop when he saw Elisabeth standing by the sofa, one hand gripping Tammy's arm, the other holding a gun pressed to the side of Tammy's head. Blood trickled from Tammy's temple.

"Don't worry. I just tapped her with the gun barrel this time," Elisabeth said. "But if you don't cooperate, I'll shoot her."

"You shot Mitch," he said.

"Am I supposed to tell you you're a clever boy because you figured that out?" She sneered. "Vin, Vin, Vinnie, Vince."

He almost staggered under the weight of the knowledge that hit him then. Elisabeth was from Omaha, Nebraska. The town where his father had seen a young woman who looked like Valerie. She had shown up in Eagle Mountain about the time the messages from V began arriving. Her hair was darker than Valerie's, but she had the same slightly up-turned nose and the same dimple in her left cheek that he had. "Valerie, what are you doing?" he asked.

"It took you long enough to recognize me. I shouldn't have to tell you how insulting it is that you didn't even know who I was. Your long-lost twin. The one you had supposedly mourned all these years. Such hypocrisy."

"What do you want from us?" he asked.

Valerie looked at Tammy. "You see how he gets right to the point? He doesn't care what I've been up to for the past fifteen years. He just wants to know the bottom line. What will it take to make me go away again?"

"That's not what I meant," he said. "And I do care—"

"Shut up! Don't waste my time with more lies. As for what I want from you, that's easy. You and Mom and Dad—mostly Mom and Dad, but I blame you too, because you were their favorite and you didn't do anything to stop them—took away my life. The life I could have had, anyway. Now you get to pay with *your* life."

Vince glanced at Tammy. She was pale, but calm. Strong. "Let Tammy go and I'll do whatever you want," he said.

"Let her go right to the sheriff? I don't think so. No, you two are the buy-one-get-one special today." She shoved Tammy onto the sofa. "Sit down over here beside your girl-friend, and we'll talk about what happens next."

Vince sat. He wanted to keep her talking. As long as she was talking, she wasn't shooting. And every word bought a lit-tle more time for the sheriff and his deputies to figure out that

Elisabeth was V. She had shot her boyfriend and come after him and his family. "Why did you shoot Mitch?" he asked.

"I've already explained everything to your girlfriend. He was in the way of what I needed to do. Is he dead yet? I figured if the bullet didn't finish him off, the fall into the canyon would."

"He's alive," Vince said. "He'll tell the cops everything."

Tammy let out a whimper. Valerie glared at her, then turned her attention back to Vince. "By the time they find me, it will be too late," she said. "I know how to change my appearance and my name and melt into the background. Paul taught me all that."

"Who is Paul?"

Valerie sighed. "Again, I've already told Tammy. I don't like repeating myself. He's the man who saved me when my *family* threw me out."

"He was the camper you saw?" Vince guessed. "The one with the blue tent?"

"Again, you're smarter than I thought. And a hero to boot, climbing mountains and descending into canyons to save complete strangers. That surprised me when I found out. You were always such a coward. Too bad you didn't try harder to save me."

He started to reply, but Tammy squeezed his hand, hard. A warning not to upset Valerie by arguing with her? He squeezed back, letting her know he got the message. "That was you in the casino in Omaha, the time Dad saw you, wasn't it?" he asked.

"He told you about that, did he? I heard he came snooping around the next day, looking for me. But the manager had a thing for me, so he didn't mind saying he didn't know anything about me. I told him the guy asking questions was a creepy old man who was hassling me."

"Was it you who made those phone calls—the ones saying 'Help me' and asking for Daddy?"

She looked away. "I don't want to talk about that anymore. Stand up, both of you." She motioned with the gun. "Time to get this show on the road."

They stood.

"Oh, isn't that sweet? You're holding hands. But don't think the two of you are going to get the better of me. I've had lots of time to think about this. Now, get into the bedroom and take off all your clothes."

He and Tammy looked at each other with a mixture of shock and confusion. "Get going," Valerie ordered. "It's not like you two haven't seen each other naked before."

They went into the bedroom. "Clothes off!" Valerie barked. "Quit wasting my time."

Vince sat on the edge of the bed and began unlacing his boots. Slowly. Instead of sitting beside him, Tammy moved to the other side of the bed and took off her earrings. Good idea. The more space between them, the more difficult it would be for Valerie to watch them both at once.

Boots off, Vince turned his attention to removing his belt. He weighed it in his hand, wondering if he could use it as a weapon.

The gunshot was deafening in the small space. He jumped up and saw that Valerie had fired into the mattress. "The next one will be right in her chest if you don't get moving," she said, pointing the gun at Tammy.

He draped the belt over the headboard, then moved more quickly, shucking his jeans and socks, then peeling off his shirt, until he was standing in front of her in his boxers. "That's enough," she said. "I can always strip the body later." She turned once more to Tammy. "You lie down on the bed. Vince, you tie her up with those scarves." She indicated two scarves draped around the bedposts. "One hand to each bed-post. And do a good job."

Tammy remained standing, also in her underwear. "Why have him tie me up?"

"I'm setting the scene. Vince, depressed over the loss of his dear little sister, kills himself. But first, he kills you. After subjecting you to kinky sex."

Valerie's love of drama hadn't changed. But he didn't see any way out of doing what she wanted. He believed her when she said the next bullet would be for Tammy.

Tammy lay back on the bed. "Sorry about this," Vince said, as he knelt beside her and picked up one of the scarves.

I love you, she mouthed, and he nodded, unable to get out any words past the lump in his throat. He tied her wrist to the bedpost, not too tight but in what he hoped was a con-vincing knot. Then he moved to the other wrist.

"Comfortable?" Valerie asked. She moved to check the wrist Vince had just tied and made a tsking sound. "As I sus-pected, not tight enough. Just for that, you're going to get an extra bullet, Vince."

The teasing tone she used enraged him. He watched out of the corner of his eye as she bent over the knot, the pistol balanced awkwardly in her right hand as she used her ring and pinkie fingers to hold the scarf in place as she tight-ened the knot.

He left the other wrist untied and grabbed hold of the belt. The heavy buckle hit Valerie hard on the cheek, draw-ing blood. She juggled the gun and it went off, but the bul-let hit the wall. Tammy yanked her hand away and rolled off the bed, landing hard on the floor. Meanwhile, Vince had lunged, both hands around the wrist that held the gun, until he succeeded in wrenching it from her. But she knocked it from his hand, and it fired again as it hit the floor.

He continued to wrestle with Valerie, struggling to subdue her. She fought with incredible strength, biting and kicking, scratching at his face and trying to knee him in the groin. Tammy raced from the room and returned a few seconds later with something in her hand. "Hold her still!" she pleaded.

But just then, Valerie bit Vince's hand, drawing blood. He drew back instinctively, and she lunged, over-balancing him. They both fell to the floor, her on top, both hands around his throat. His vision blurred, and he was sure he would black out.

Then he heard a horrible sound, like a knife cleaving a watermelon. Valerie's grip loosened, and she fell to one side.

Tammy stood over them, spattered with blood, the ice ax from Vince's search and rescue pack in her hand.

Pounding on the door reverberated through the house. "This is the sheriff!" Travis shouted. "Come out with your hands up!"

Tammy dropped the ax, and Vince staggered to his feet. He put his arm around her. "Come on," he said.

"I can't go out there like this," she whispered.

He reached back and grabbed the top sheet from the bed and wrapped it around her, then took the bottom sheet for himself. They walked into the living room just as the door burst open and Gage and Travis entered.

Gage took in the bedclothes and their state of undress and frowned. "We had a report of multiple gunshots at this address," he said. "And Mitch Patterson's car is outside in the lot. We believe his girlfriend, Elisabeth Rollins, tried to kill him."

"His girlfriend is in the bedroom," Vince said. "She shot Mitch, then tried to kill us. And her name isn't Elisabeth Rollins. It's Valerie Shepherd."

Jamie Douglas stepped in behind the Walker brothers. "You two can come with me," she said.

Tammy was shaking by the time they reached the parking lot, though the temperature was mild. Her eyes were glazed, her skin cold and clammy. "Call an ambulance," Vince said. "I think she's going into shock."

"One is on the way," Jamie said. "I've got a sweatshirt and pants in my patrol vehicle you can put on, Tammy, and Gage will have something that will fit you, Vince." She retrieved the clothes from the back of her SUV and started to help Tammy unwind the sheet when she saw the blood spatters. "Are you hurt?" she asked.

"That isn't my blood," Tammy said. "It's Valerie's." Then she broke down sobbing.

Vince gathered her close while Jamie radioed this information to Travis. More deputies arrived, along with an ambulance and most of Vince's neighbors. Tammy's boss, camera in hand, showed up. Vince only vaguely registered their presence. He held on to Tammy, smoothing her hair and murmuring, "It's going to be all right," over and over. As if by repetition, he could make himself believe it.

TAMMY SPENT THE night in the hospital, with Vince on one side of her bed and her mother on the other. She hadn't wanted to stay here, but the doctor had insisted it was necessary, then given her a sedative that made her not care anymore.

When she finally woke, sun streamed through the one window in her room. Vince got up from the chair where he had been sitting and came to the side of the bed. "How are you feeling?" he asked.

"I'm okay." She reached up and touched the bruise on the side of her face. It was tender, but the doctors had reassured her there was no lasting damage. She trembled when she thought of how much worse it could have been. "How are you?"

"Shaken up. But I'm going to be okay."

She turned to look at the chair where her mother had sat. "She went down to see your brother," Vince said.

Her eyes widened as she remembered Mitch. He had been in surgery when they installed her in this room last night. "Is he going to be okay?"

"He's got a long recovery ahead of him. Another surgery to pin his leg together. But he's going to be okay."

"And Valerie?"

"She's alive. You didn't kill her. You merely gave her a concussion. And saved both our lives."

Tammy's eyes filled with tears. "Your poor parents."

A tap on the door frame interrupted their discussion. Sheriff Travis Walker entered. "I stopped by to see how you're doing," he said.

"I'm going to be fine," Tammy said.

"I was just down getting a statement from your brother."

"What did he say?" Vince asked.

"He says the woman he knew as Elisabeth asked him to stop the car by the side of the road because she was feeling sick. Earlier in the day, she had surprised him with the news that she was pregnant, so he thought that was the reason she was feeling ill. He helped her over to the edge of the road. She pulled out a gun, shot him and pushed him over the edge."

"Cold blooded," Vince said.

"Vince has already given me his statement," Travis said. "Can you tell me what happened before he arrived at the condo yesterday evening?"

Tammy smoothed her hands over the sheets and tried to gather her thoughts. "I'll try to remember everything," she said.

Travis took out a recorder, recited her name and his and the time and date. Then she proceeded to tell her story, reliving those horrible moments when Valerie told her about Mitch and threatened her own life and that of Vince and the Shepherds. Vince held her hand while she spoke, keeping her strong. When she was finished, Travis shut off the recorder. "What will happen to Valerie?" she asked.

"She's in custody now but will be transferred to a mental health unit soon," Travis said. "The court will determine if she stands trial for the arson and three counts of attempted murder. Not to mention the thousands and thousands of dollars she and Paul Rollins have stolen over the years."

"Did you find out anything about Paul Rollins?" Vince asked.

"He was a former school teacher in Ogallala, Nebraska. He was fired after accusations of improper conduct with a student. A nine-year-old girl. He left town and fell off the radar for nine months, until he showed up with a girl he called Elisabeth. He introduced her as his daughter. They're suspected of being involved in various con games all over the country, in Mexico and the Caribbean. They targeted wealthy, older people with either investment or charity schemes. He apparently used Valerie to lull his targets into trusting him."

"Valerie said he was dead," Tammy said.

"He died two months ago of an asthma attack," Travis said. "He had a history of the disease, but when I contacted authorities in Omaha, I learned they are considering opening an investigation into his death."

"Do they think Valerie killed him?" Vince asked.

"I don't know," Travis said.

"She scares me," Tammy admitted.

"Whether she stands trial for the things she's done or is

committed for treatment, she won't be free to live on her own for a long time, if ever," Travis said.

"I'm trying to remind myself that she was hurt by what happened too," Tammy said. "Whatever this Paul guy did to her, it damaged her mind. I don't know if someone can ever come back from that."

"My parents are determined to help her any way they can," Vince said. "She's still their daughter, and they're relieved to know what happened to her, even if it hasn't resulted in the happy ending they're hoping for."

"One day, maybe she'll realize how fortunate she is to have them on her side," Travis said. He pocketed the recorder. "You'll need to stop by the office in the next day or so to sign this statement. And we may have other questions for both of you."

"Of course."

"Your condo will be unavailable for a few days," Travis said. "I can give you the name of a company that will clean it for you before you move back in."

"Okay," Vince said. "Thanks."

Travis took something from his pocket. Tammy thought it would be a business card for the cleaning company. Instead, he handed Vince a key. "You'll need a place to stay for a few days," he said. "Someplace quiet, away from the press and nosy neighbors. I have a cabin you can use. Up on Spirit Ridge. It's nothing fancy, but it's comfortable."

Vince stared at the key. "Thanks."

Travis left and Vince pocketed the key. "That was nice of him," Tammy said.

"He's a good man," Vince said. "He'll do right by Valerie, whether she deserves it or not."

"That cabin sounds like exactly what we need," she said. "When can I leave?"

"Whenever you want, I think," he said.

She looked toward the door. "I'd like to see Mitch, and I should say goodbye to my mother. What if she wants me to stay with her?"

"The hospital has an arrangement with a nearby hotel," he said. "She'll stay there until your brother transfers to a rehab facility."

She lay back on the pillows once more. "What a nightmare," she said.

He sat on the side of the bed and took her hand. "It will be a while before I can forget the sight of my sister standing there with a gun to your head," he said. "I came so close to losing you."

"You didn't lose me." She sat up and pulled him close. "And as awful as the next few months or years might be at times, you don't have to go through all this alone now."

"I know," he said. "That's the best thing to come out of all of this. Whatever happens, we'll get through it together."

Nothing he could have said would have meant more to her. She had broken off her relationship with Darrell because he wouldn't make a commitment. She didn't need a marriage proposal to believe Vince would be there for her. She trusted the connection they had would grow. They both knew loss, but out of that shared knowledge, they had found so much.

* * * * *

*Look for the final book in Cindi Myers miniseries,
Eagle Mountain: Criminal History, when*
Mountain Captive *goes on sale next month.*

*And if you missed the previous
titles in the series, you'll find*
Mile High Mystery *and* Colorado Kidnapping
wherever Harlequin Intrigue books are sold!

HARLEQUIN
Reader Service

Enjoyed your book?

Try the perfect subscription for Romance readers and get more great books like this delivered right to your door.

See why over 10+ million readers have tried Harlequin Reader Service.

Start with a Free Welcome Collection with free books and a gift—valued over $20.

Choose any series in print or ebook. See website for details and order today:

TryReaderService.com/subscriptions